# Missing Letters

# MISSING LETTERS

## A Novel

*For Bens & Sno,*
*Steve Hayes*
*August, 2015*

STEPHEN HAYES

**MISSING LETTERS**
**A NOVEL**

iUniverse books may be ordered through booksellers or by contacting:

iUniverse
1663 Liberty Drive
Bloomington, IN 47403
www.iuniverse.com
1-800-Authors (1-800-288-4677)

ISBN: 978-1-4917-7043-6 (sc)
ISBN: 978-1-4917-7044-3 (e)

Library of Congress Control Number: 2015910060

Print information available on the last page.

iUniverse rev. date: 6/30/2015

"Through many dangers, toil and snares,
I have already come;
'Tis grace hath brought me safe thus far,
And grace will lead me home."

Amazing Grace
John Newton
1779

"Give up to grace. The ocean takes care of each wave until it gets to shore. You need more help than you know."

Rumi
13th century Persian poet

# BEACH WALK

*It was a glorious dawn. The eastern sky beyond the sea, a soft collage of pastels, was preparing itself for the rising of the sun. Trav and Martha and Sam walked barefoot together, as they had many times before, down the beach along the surf line. Each, coincidentally, had donned khaki Bermuda shorts. Trav's hair, mostly grey now, was without cover. Sam wore the usual faded blue Atlanta Braves baseball cap, and Martha, her favorite: a wide-brimmed straw sun hat with a bright green band of ribbon.*

*"Are you sure you have to go home?" Sam asked.*

*Martha laughed and reached her arm over Sam's shoulders.*

*"Unfortunately, we do. Maybe one of these years, we'll come down and just never go back."*

*Trav stopped to pick up a broken shell. He examined it briefly, then flung it out to sea. "That's a capital idea," he said. As he watched his missile arc out over the ocean and splash, he recalled that after his first tumultuous trip to the island, he really did not expect to return. In fact, he and Martha had since come together for ten consecutive Augusts, always staying at the same remote, ramshackle, two-bedroom cottage on the beach and always spending lots of time with Sam Brewer.*

*"How many times," Sam mused, "have I thought about that first year when Trav came down here by himself."*

*Martha craned her head to the sky. "Oh, mercy. What a time that was. Sometimes I can't believe we actually got through it." Trav looked over at his wife as she and Sam walked step for step in the ankle-deep surf. He saw in her face, in the crow's feet around her eyes, a hint of the toll that year had taken on her, a toll that was masked, although not entirely,* by her current countenance. They walked north, the gentle waves lapping and sloshing around their legs.

As they rounded a curve in the coastline, Trav pointed ahead. "There's my sweet girl."

The old sloop was nestled hard against a sand dune, her hull faded, but smooth, her single mast pointing proudly to the heavens. Trav closed his eyes for a moment, recalling his first time on this beach and his encounter with that sturdy little boat that had changed his life. He remembered too what had preceded his first visit and what had propelled him down the Atlantic coast and onto the Island. His bare feet imprinted the cool, wet sand at the water's edge. That year, he thought, that incredible, terrible year. A remnant of the old feelings of loss and fear and powerlessness moved in his chest.

They turned and headed south, back to the cottage for breakfast. The first golden slice of sun peeked above the horizon, heralding one more day.

# CHAPTER 1

## Explosion at Home

The airborne chair exploded through the bay window, sending shards of glass and splintered mullions out into the garden.

The boy screamed, "Go to hell! Go to hell, all of you! You don't tell me what to do!" "I'm your mother, Daniel," Martha said, feeling both fury and fear. It took a few seconds, but the fury overwhelmed the fear. "I'm your mother and I can tell you this, young man. You have just lost your right to live in this house!"

Daniel glared wild-eyed at his mother. "This isn't a house. It's a torture chamber. You and Dad don't have a..."

She cut him off. "Leave now! I just need you to leave."

The teenager grabbed his jacket, swung it over his shoulder in a wide, angry arc and stormed out of the family room toward the front door.

"I'm outa here alright. Never coming back. Bye, bitch!"

Martha heard the door slam hard. She heard the car engine start, then the squeal of the tires on the driveway. She stood expressionless, motionless, empty in the aching silence of her broken life. A cold October breeze flowed in through the windowless bay and pressed lightly on her face. She closed her eyes, then opened them, hoping she might look out on a different world. But it was the same, the very same. She sat on the couch. Slowly, ever so slowly, she lowered her face into her trembling hands. Then came the sobs of anguish and heartache.

"Oh, God," she moaned. "Oh, God help us....please help us."

❧❧

The front door opened, but Martha had not heard it.

"Hello?" Footsteps in the hall.

"Hello? Martha?"

Trav came to the end of the hallway, taking the single step down into the family room. "Martha, are you...oh my God, what...what in the world?" He moved quickly to the sofa, sat and put his arm around his wife. He asked her what had happened. Martha lifted her head and turned her wet face toward her husband.

"Trav, I can't do this anymore. I can't."

Trav scanned the room. "Did Daniel...?"

"I came home," Martha said, almost in a whisper. "He was asleep in the basement. It's two in the afternoon, for God's sake. I called down, told him he needed to go to the clinic for his drug test. It was the usual. He stalled. He fell back asleep. Finally, he comes up. He's surly. We argued about something. I don't even remember what now. But all of a sudden, he went ballistic. Just went nuts. And then he..." Martha finished the sentence with a defeated, open-handed wave to the chair outside cantilevered on top of a large azalea.

The ensuing silence was the silence of cold stone. Then Martha spoke again. "I told him he had to leave."

"Leave?" Trav's face was pained. "He's only seventeen. Where will he go?"

Martha gazed out at her garden-turned-war zone. "I have no idea. Stay with friends probably. All I know is that we have to stop this insanity and..."

"But he's our son, Martha."

"He is. But he is also a drug addict, a liar, a thief and a one-man wrecking crew."

Trav started, "But we can't just..."

Martha turned sharply and cut him off. "And you bought him that damned car and you give him money!"

"Just for gas."

"Oh, please! Open your eyes. He gets money from you and then he siphons gas from your car at night. He's buying drugs."

2

"You don't know that."

"I do know it!" Martha shouted. "I do know it, damn it! I do know it! You tell him something. You tell me something else. Then you cave. How is it you had enough courage to spend two years in Vietnam, but you don't have enough to deny Daniel twenty dollars when you know what he's going to do with it?"

Martha sat looking into her lap for a long time, then spoke, now quietly, firmly, without inflection. "I feel all alone in this. All alone." She took a deep breath. "I think you're afraid of Daniel. You're afraid to be his father."

Trav stood. He surveyed the damage before him and looked quietly down at Martha, who was now motionless, her wet eyes closed, her head resting on the back of the sofa. Even in her current state of deep distress, he saw the beauty he had married. Her lustrous auburn hair, her gentle face and, in his mind's eye, he saw her soft brown doe eyes. He quietly turned toward the back door that opened to Martha's garden. Outside, he carefully lifted the chair off the azalea and placed it carefully under the eave overhanging the back door.

Their property backed up to a small county park that lay in the center of the neighborhood. The walking path in the park was a meandering half-mile circle. He stepped gingerly through his wife's garden to the rear property line, ducked slightly under a drooping pine branch and stepped into the woods. It was, for him, a very familiar routine. Often, all too often, his anger and fear had led him into the woods, running—actually, walking—away from problems. And so he pushed through the light underbrush to the mulched path. The autumn leaves, those clinging to their branches and those already on the ground, were all a soft, quiet yellow.

Spear's house was just beyond the first curve. Trav thought of stopping to share with his friend the disastrous events of the past hour. He stopped at his back gate and saw him through the den window, pipe in hand, reading by the fire. Every time he was with Spear, Trav thought of Carl Sandburg reading his poetry that windy winter day when John F. Kennedy was inaugurated. Spear, he thought, has that Sandburg thick shock of unruly white hair falling over his forehead, that same weathered face, and those same wise, experienced eyes.

Spear knew so much, yet he read vociferously, always wanting to learn more.

Trav wanted now to sit with him and talk quietly. But he would not. Not today. He needed to go home. He needed to be there for Martha.

# CHAPTER 2

## Third and Last Session with the Shrink

He looked at Dr. Ramos, then glanced past him to the small wooden desk with its pile of folders, two prescription pads and, beyond the papers, a framed certificate of award from the U.S. Department of Veteran Affairs. Next to the certificate was a photograph of a woman and a young boy, the psychiatrist's wife and son, Trav presumed.

"Well, Trav," the doctor began quietly. "how has your week been?"

"Not bad," Trav said, "considering our seventeen-year-old son screamed obscenities at my wife, threw a chair through our bay window and ran away."

"Oh my gosh," said Ramos.

"Yeah," Trav said, adding sarcastically, "Other than that, just a great week."

And so began Traveler McGale's third session with the Veterans Affairs trauma counselor.

ജ്ഞ

He and Martha had been married twenty-seven years and had built a reasonably good life together. Nice home in a suburban area just west of Philadelphia, a vintage 1930s stone house with a weathered slate roof. A previous owner had torn down the old one-car garage in the back and constructed in its place a new, high-ceiling family room. They had two cars. Two kids. For Trav, a modestly successful practice with a small law firm, Stephens and Tate, and for Martha, a part time teaching position at a local private school.

Until now, life had been, well, not too bad. Early in their marriage, Trav would tell Martha about his dreams—his nightmares—of the war. Later, the bad dreams became tiresomely repetitive, so he just stopped talking about them. But Martha continued to be on the receiving end of his periodic bursts of anger, his times when he *went away*, not literally. It was just that sometimes when he was with her, he was somewhere else.

And then there was the drinking. Trav was not a drunk. In fact, he was almost never truly drunk and he only drank after work, at least as far as Martha knew. But he drank every day and more than she wanted to see.

She suggested one day that he might try a few counseling sessions, choosing wisely not to mention the alcohol issue, but gently raising instead Trav's restlessness and occasional sadness. Martha made her case delicately, but he didn't buy it, at least not at first. She floated the idea once or twice more with no apparent effect. One day, though, Trav exploded over something trivial, threw his coffee mug into the sink and stormed off to the office, leaving Martha to clean up the shattered mug and splattered coffee. At home that evening, he casually mentioned that he had called the VA and made an appointment.

❦

Dr. Ramos bounced the back end of his pen against his note pad. "I'm sorry to hear those developments about your son."

Trav didn't respond.

The psychiatrist cleared his throat. "Well, I'm certainly glad you're back. Let's see." he continued, looking down at his notes, "In our first two sessions, last week and the week before, you told me about your time in Vietnam. You were with the Marines up near the demilitarized zone, you said."

Dr. Ramos paused, removed his reading glasses and looked up at Trav. "I am hoping you and I can make some discoveries together."

Trav puckered his lips, filled his cheeks with air and rhythmically tapped his finger tips on the wooden arm chair rests. He was on guard. *Is this the way shrinks work?*

"Discoveries,huh?"

"Yes. Maybe we'll dig up some hidden treasure. Maybe we won't."

Trav looked at his doctor with a challenging give-it-your-best-shot-buddy stare and said nothing.

The counselor looked away and regarded the wet melting snow outside his office window. Still studying the world outside, he said, "You know, it's been my observation over the years that we humans are motivated, by and large, by love or fear."

Another lingering silence.

The doctor reached with both hands for a cup of tea sitting by his side. He blew tiny ripples onto the surface of the dark liquid and then spoke again. "Yes. Love and fear. They are our two big drivers. What do you think about that, Trav?"

"Never really thought about it," Trav said. "Makes sense, I guess."

"So," the doctor said, "what do you love, Trav?"

Trav uncrossed and recrossed his legs, then crossed his arms over his chest. He pondered the question for a moment, then answered, "Well, I love Martha. I love my kids."

"What else?"

"I love being on the golf course. I love a good steak. I love a good glass of wine."

"And what do you fear?"

Trav looked up at the ceiling. He said nothing. The doctor studied him and probed from a new, actually, an old, direction.

"We've talked in here about the war..."

"Oh, come on, Doc. Let's..."

"Do you want to tell me...?"

"We've already plowed through all that. I've told you about my tours, the firefights, and the stuff at night. What happened to Vince. Why do we have to rummage through all that again?"

The doctor again gently blew over his tea. "We don't *have* to do anything. It's your hour."

"Fifty minutes,." Trav reminded him.

"Yes. Fifty minutes."

The psychiatrist made a few notes, then looked up.

"You're right. We talked about the war. You told me about the valley and that one night especially. It's been, what, almost thirty years? But you still have a lot of energy around all that. You get emotional. Last week, it seemed you wanted to talk about it. Today, I think you don't."

Trav shrugged. It was now his turn to watch the melting snow.

"So," Dr. Ramos said, "if you care to, talk to me about what you feel when you feel Vietnam."

Trav's mouth dropped open. "When I feel Vietnam?" He repeated the question. "When I feel Vietnam? What the hell are you talking about?"

"You talk about Vietnam from time to time. You think about it, I'm sure. You told me you used to have recurring nightmares. I'm simply asking. When memories of the war enter your mind, what do you feel?"

Trav put a curled fist under his chin and thought about the question. For a minute, actually for several of his allotted fifty minutes, he sat very still, staring unblinkingly at the small oval Oriental rug at his feet. Finally, he started his answer. "I guess I feel angry and also...." He stopped.

"And also?" the doctor queried.

Trav shifted in his chair and stretched his legs out, putting the soles of both shoes on the carpet. "And also sad."

"Sad because?"

"Sad because I lost my good, young years. Because I will know for the rest of my life that I spent those years risking my ass for a mistake. Sad because a bunch of my friends don't even have a rest of their life."

Dr. Ramos closed his notebook, placed his reading glasses on the table next to his tea and said, "I'm afraid our time is almost..."

But Trav was back on the other side of the world and he wasn't finished.

"And I'm sad because I thought the world was a friendly place." He looked at the psychiatrist square on and the doctor returned his gaze. A soft wave of sadness passed across his patient's face. Trav swallowed. He felt he was entering a kind of trance. From a place unknown, deep within, he heard himself saying, "I still have a picture of the world as a friendly place. You ask what I love. It's that picture. That's what I love.

8

But anymore, I can't really see it very well. Life keeps coming at me and hurting and breaking the picture into pieces."

Dr. Ramos did not respond. Trav suddenly felt very tired. He slumped back into his chair and closed his eyes, with his thumb and forefinger lightly pinching the bridge of his nose. He was aware of the doctor thinking his patient was going to break and sob as he reached for the ever-present box of tissues. Pen in one hand, tissue box in the other, he paused, motionless.

With Trav too, there was no motion; nor were there tears. He looked up again.

"You know, doc, I think my problem isn't Vietnam. My problem is my silly belief that the war was an exceptional intrusion into an otherwise happy world."

The psychiatrist put the tissue box back alongside the mug of tea and the glasses.

Trav continued. "Bits of happiness are the exceptional intrusions. The world is basically fucked up. Why did it take me so many years to figure that out?"

There was a soft knock on the door. The doctor turned his head and spoke over his shoulder, "In just a minute." He turned back. "We have to stop for today, but I want you to know I hear you and I validate what you said. You did good work."

As he left the doctor's office, Trav looked at this watch. *Sixty-three minutes. What a bargain.*

After he had started seeing Dr. Ramos, Trav began reading about post-traumatic stress disorder, PTSD. He thought that with the counseling sessions, *it* would go away. He thought that by "going back there," as the doctor put it, by talking openly about the war, that the fear and the anger and the sadness would fade. But that had not happened. Instead, Traveler not only moved more acutely into his memories, but the emotional turbulence surfaced more from the deep and rolled ever more heavily into his days.

Those memories were not of a whole cloth. They were raw bits of disjointed char, random clips from an old movie that had been racked on the reel and watched too many times. The private from Oklahoma, gung-ho—too gung-ho—who crawled out beyond the perimeter one night and took a round through his night vision scope that blew off the back of his head. Trav had cradled the boy—and he was a boy—as he carried him through the thundering din of that brutal field. He remembers the arms hanging limp and the one remaining eye with its lifeless stare out to eternity. The random clip from another day when their medic, who stood, only to receive a B-40 rocket through his sternum. And he remembered Vince Lanzinita and the jokes and the warm beer they shared the night before he died. Trav remembered his helo ride out of the mountains to Saigon and his relief to be heading home and later his stinging guilt of leaving those in the mountains who would one day head home in a box.

No. No. For sure, it did not go away. Like a cunning cat, it would silently slip off into the tall grass, only to reappear without warning and nestle once again behind his heart.

# CHAPTER 3
## Evening Respite

Trav put the cassette tape in the player. It was the score from the movie, *Corelli's Mandolin*, which was just out in theaters. He never understood quite why, but for some reason that music touched him, moved him deeply and transported him, if only briefly, to a place of serenity. Normally, waiting for dinner, he would have a newspaper or legal brief in his lap. But this evening, he simply sat. He liked the music. He liked the garden view outside the newly replaced bay window. He liked the aroma of Martha's fresh baked lasagna wafting from the kitchen. But most of all, he liked that feeling of serenity.

While waiting for her lasagna to cool, Martha looked into the family room and at her husband. His hair, a rich brownish red when they had married, had turned more salt and pepper grey. His body, grown somewhat thicker with age, was still the physique of the strong young athlete he once was.

Trav looked up with his blue Celtic eyes and saw Martha regarding him.

"Supper's almost ready," she said.

"Smell's wonderful," Trav said, rising and walking toward the kitchen.

After what the couple started referring to as the 'Day of the Flying Chair,' Daniel disappeared, bunking in, they learned later, with friends. Trav and Martha talked, almost, it seemed, to the point of exhaustion, about what to do. Run after their son and bring him home? Leave him alone and let him learn the hard way? They had talked about asking the police to search for Daniel's car, but tabled the idea. Three weeks went by with no communication in spite of Trav's repeated calls and texts to Daniel's cell phone.

During their dinner, it had started to rain outside. The meal finished, Martha was cleaning up in the kitchen when the doorbell rang. Trav went to the front door and opened it as the bell chimed for a second time. There in the gloom of a cold evening rain stood young Daniel McGale. He was shorter than his father, but only by a few inches. His reddish-brown hair, now wet and matted from the rain, fell over his ears and forehead, almost to his eyebrows. He had always been thin but was now even more so. He regarded his father through dull brown eyes. For a moment, the two simply looked at one another. Daniel's breath clouded in the cold, wet air.

"Hi."

"Hi," Trav said flatly.

Martha called from the kitchen, "Who is it?"

Trav didn't respond to his wife. Instead he said softly, "Come in."

Again from the kitchen. "Who is it, Trav?"

"It's Daniel."

The young man was not a pretty sight. Trav surveyed his scraggly, unshaven face, his tired eyes, a dirty shirttail visible under his even dirtier jacket. The boy walked ahead of his father through the dining room into the kitchen. He looked warily at his mother.

"Hey," he said.

"Hey to you," said Martha, forcing herself to hold in abeyance her relief and the passel of questions a mother wanted to ask.

Daniel looked briefly at his father, then to his mother again, shoving his hands deep into his pockets. He looked at the kitchen floor.

Silence.

Finally, Martha asked quietly, "Are you hungry?"

"Yeah. Kinda."

She retrieved the lasagna that had just been stored in the refrigerator, cut a large square and poured a glass of milk. Trav watched Daniel eat. He was relieved to see him. He was angry at him. He was at a loss for what to say or do.

Later, the three of them sat together in the family room. Daniel glanced briefly at the bay window, then turned his attention to the meal he had just consumed.

"That was good lasagna," he said, not looking up

And so began the long conversation, haltingly at first, then with a more fulsome flow. Daniel admitted to drug use, but concealed the extent of it. He admitted to drinking, but again concealed the extent. He said he wanted to go back to school. His parents, of course, had had their own conversations about Daniel since his disappearance. Trav wanted him back home. Martha knew that would not work. They had discussed drug and alcohol rehabilitation and they had discussed boarding schools. Their strategy had remained 'under discussion' when the doorbell rang that night.

Martha went back to the kitchen for more lasagna and milk for her son. She dawdled and delayed, opening the refrigerator, then closing it, then opening it again, playing for time, thinking, trying to settle on her next move. She wanted to sit down with Trav and talk, just the two of them, about what to do. But now, without warning, it was the three of them. Daniel was tired and, she thought, somewhat submissive. She had to seize the moment.

Lasagna in one hand, a large glass of milk in the other, she gingerly navigated the single step down into the family room. Crossing the room, she took a deep breath, handed the plate and glass to her son and plunged in.

"Daniel," she said, looking directly at him, "we love you. We love you more than you know and I appreciate your honesty. It's good to hear you open up." She paused and looked over at Trav, then turned back. "But you just can't live here right now. It's not that...your father and I..." She started to lose her words and her nerve, but steadied herself and regained her resolve. "Your father and I have decided to give you a choice. You can either go to a rehab program or to a special school that we have..."

Daniel broke in. "What! I'm not going to any damned rehab! No! I told you. I admitted that I....I can handle this. No! My friends are here."

*Sure,* Martha thought, *your drug friends.* Meanwhile, Trav, staring at Martha, was speechless. *What had she just said? What the...?*

13

The three of them talked well into the night. Trav gradually found himself supporting Martha's peremptory diktat. Daniel gradually found himself testing and probing the edges of his two options. By midnight, Daniel was too tired to continue the conversation.

"Go on to bed," Trav said, desperate for sleep himself. "Sleep on all this. We'll talk tomorrow.

# CHAPTER 4

## *Up to Maine*

Two weeks later, as the cooling airs of November began to envelop Pennsylvania, Daniel was enrolled in Burson-Mann, a coeducational boarding high school in Maine. According to the school's brochure, Burson-Mann "specializes in educating young adults with legal and/or addiction issues and/or learning or behavioral differences." Trav thought the description fit pretty much every teenager on the planet. Martha thought the institution would be a good fit for their son. Daniel thought 'whatever.'

Trav and Martha had another child, Eryn, three years older than Daniel. Compared with her brother, Eryn had been a joy to raise. She was pretty. She was smart and she was, at least so far, a junior in college, moving well through her young life. Trim and athletic-looking, her hair, lighter and redder than her brother's, was almost always in a long ponytail. A spirinkling of Irish freckles rested under her bright blue eyes. Eryn came home for Thanksgiving that month and the McGale home held all the outward appearances of normalcy. Brother and sister chatted amiably a bit. They each spent some time with their respective friends.

On Thanksgiving morning, Martha, her blue apron covering her dress, labored happily in the kitchen stuffing the turkey, warming the gravy on the stove and stirring her mashed sweet potatoes. Trav had wanted to watch a four o'clock football game on television and Martha had promised him they would eat promptly at three. They sat at the dining room table. Martha extended her arms. The four McGales held hands as Martha and Eryn closed their eyes. Trav and Daniel bowed their heads, staring unblinkingly at the feast before them. Martha prayed, "Lord, make us thankful for these and all our many blessings. Amen."

The mealtime conversation was light, a bit stilted. How is school going, Eryn? Need to get raking the leaves next week. Martha said she was glad they were all together.

As she stood to clear the table, Eryn said, "So, bro, you're heading up to Maine, are you?"

Daniel took a swallow of his milk. "Yep, looks like it."

Eryn handed her empty plate to her mother and turned back to Daniel. "Well, good luck up there. Stay in touch, huh?"

"Sure."

And that was it. The elephant in the room was fleetingly acknowledged and the family shifted smoothly back to their pleasant Thanksgiving chatter about nothing in particular. Martha called from the kitchen, "Who wants ice cream on their pumpkin pie?"

◌◌◌

Eryn headed back to school early the Sunday after Thanksgiving. Shortly after she left, Trav, Martha and Daniel headed north in the family Honda. The following morning, the three of them were sitting in the headmaster's office at Burson-Mann Academy.

"Daniel," asked Mr. O'Malley, "do you prefer Dan, Daniel, Danny?"

"Anything's okay. Daniel, I guess."

The headmaster said, "I'm a Daniel too. Dan to my friends. But you will only need to remember Mr. O'Malley."

Daniel, the younger, looked at Daniel, the elder, silently taking the measure of his new superior, observing his tweed jacket with leather elbow patches, the forest green V-neck sweater, his pale, ice-blue eyes and his greying reddish hair. An elderly black Labrador lay sleeping on a throw rug in the corner of the office.

"So, Daniel," said Mr. O'Malley, "What brought you here to Burson-Mann?"

Daniel pointed out the window. "That silver Honda Pilot."

Trav snapped, "Hey, pal, let's not start with the snide stuff." He paused, looking sternly at his son. "You want to start again?"

Daniel shifted in his seat, crossed his arms and changed course. "Well, my parents suggested it. I've been not going to school for a while. Been dealing with some stuff."

"Yes, I gathered," said the headmaster, opening a manila folder in the middle of his otherwise bare mahogany desk. He reached in his breast pocket for his rimless reading glasses and perused the contents of the folder. "I've got your transcript here. Interesting. Ninth and tenth grades you were a pretty good student. Very good, actually. And for the first half of eleventh grade too. Then last spring, you started downhill. And this fall so far, Fs and Incompletes." Mr. O'Malley raised his glasses, lodging them on his forehead. "What happened?"

Daniel returned the headmaster's direct gaze and held the optical stand-off. Then he answered, "Drugs."

Martha and Trav both looked stunned, hearing their son's calm candor.

"Ah, yes," said Mr. O'Malley, "so it was not really the Honda Pilot that has brought us together."

"Yeah, I guess not."

"Well, you are not alone here. There are lots of young boys and girls up here who are in your shoes exactly. Boys and girls who are changing and growing. Boys and girls who are becoming young men and women."

Trav said, "Mr. O'Malley, we are very grateful that you would accept Daniel here on such short notice in the middle of the school year."

"We're pleased that we could accommodate you," the headmaster responded. "This is not an ordinary school. And frankly, for us, this kind of admission is not out of the ordinary."

O'Malley turned back to his new student. "Daniel, this is a chance for you, an opportunity to turn your life around. Do you want to turn your life around?"

Daniel fidgeted with the zipper on his winter jacket.

"Yeah. I guess."

Trav glared at his son. *I guess? You are a young man sinking fast. You have a chance to really change your life. And you guess?*

The headmaster started on the rules, as he had a thousand times before.

"To be successful here, you only need to follow three simple rules. Just three." He looked as sternly as possible at Daniel.

"Rule One: Obey school rules. Rule Two: Be honest. Rule Three: Do your best. Got it, young man?"

Daniel, his demeanor somewhere between a deer caught in the headlights and a defiant don't-push-me stare, said, barely audibly, "Got it."

O'Malley then turned his attention to Trav and Martha and said, "And if you have not done so already, I strongly recommend you both attend Al Anon meetings regularly.

"Al Anon?" Trav queried.

"Yes. It's for loved ones of addicts. Check it out. It's very important."

With that, the next chapter in the life of the McGale family saga began. Martha gave Daniel a hug.

"I love you" she whispered behind his ear.

"Love you too," Daniel mumbled.

Trav put his arm around his son. "You're in capable hands here. You be good."

As Trav backed the car out of the parking space, Martha rolled down her window and waved. But Daniel had already turned his back and was walking next to Mr. O'Malley toward the boys' dormitory.

❧❦

A freezing rain in the Philadelphia area had turned to snow as darkness fell. It was Friday. Trav's work week was behind him and he was looking forward to the weekend, regardless of the weather. With his head resting on the back of the family room sofa, eyes closed, he was reliving their trip to the school. Knowing where Daniel was and knowing, or at least having a reason to hope, that he was doing well, allowed him to feel more at ease and to feel less fear. The *Corelli's Mandolin* tape was on its second replay. Martha 's call from the kitchen brought him back.

"Dinner will be ready in about five minutes."

"Okay."

Like many married couples, Trav and Martha had slipped into a kind of code language way of talking over the years. "Dinner will be ready in about five minutes" really meant "Please set the table and put spoons out for us even though we won't be using them. I want a knife and fork and spoon at each setting."

Trav never understood the unused spoon concept, but had long since stopped asking about it. He had also stopped asking why she, a devout Christian, wanted him, a mushy agnostic-cum-universalist, to say grace at the evening meal. Maybe it had to do with her old-fashioned sense of the man as head of the household. Or maybe she thought if he said grace often enough, some of the spiritual sentiment might actually seep into him.

When it was just the two of them, they ate at the small table in the family room. Martha bowed her head and reached for his hand. Trav closed her hand in his and closed his eyes. Remembering his childhood with his friends, he was tempted to say, "Good bread, good meat, good God, let's eat." Instead, he said out loud, "God bless this food and those who are about to partake. Bless this family, especially Eryn and Daniel and also one another. Amen."

Martha whispered, "Amen." She opened her eyes and reached across the table for the wooden salad bowl. "Have some."

"Thanks," Trav said, "Hard to believe, isn't it, it was only six weeks ago we were in this room, cold air coming in through the window, both of us basket cases. Who could imagine?"

"Right," said Martha. "Who could imagine how out of the ordinary an ordinary, quiet dinner could seem."

Trav swallowed a mouthful of baked cod. "I hope Daniel is getting along alright up there."

Martha reached again for the salad bowl. "So do I. I still think we should have put him in a rehab program straight away. He's an addict. He said so himself."

Trav chewed his fish for a minute. "The school has rehab as part of their operation and it's a self-contained campus. Besides, we agreed he needs to finish school. It's only until June. Then he will have his degree. Hopefully, they will have gotten him clean. Then he can go on."

"Go on to what?" Martha asked.

"Go on to the rest of his life. College maybe. At least junior college."

Martha toyed with the bits of salad on her plate. "I don't know," she said. "I just don't know."

"I know this," said Trav, "It's just a relief to know Daniel is in a safe place and for once to have an evening. A nice quiet evening."

After dinner, they settled on the couch, she with a cup of tea, he with another glass of wine, and watched a movie on television.

# CHAPTER 5

## *Spear*

The following day, Trav walked the circle path through the park for his pre-arranged lunch with Spear, their "secret male bonding repasts," as Martha referred to them. The air had turned cold overnight, but the sky was a cloudless blue. He stepped off the mulched path onto the still wet, leaf-covered ground and headed for his friend's back gate. Spear, alone now and retired, had taken up cooking, both as a hobby and as a bit of necessity. Stepping through the back door into his friend's den, Trav smelled beef stew and homemade corn bread.

"Ah, a meal fit for a king," he said, tossing his jacket over the back of a chair.

"Nothing but the finest for the Barrister," Spear replied as he emerged from the kitchen. His faded khaki pants were rumpled. His button-down white dress shirt, out of place for a Saturday at home lunch, matched the snowy color of his thick hair.

The pine-paneled den was small and cozy. They sat where they always sat: in overstuffed chairs facing the fireplace. Burning logs popped and crackled softly. Two wine glasses shouldered an open bottle of California cabernet that stood on a rough hewn oak coffee table. Spear poured. Trav lightly touched his glass to Spear's.

"Cheers."

"Cheers."

Spear sipped his wine, then said, "Days are getting shorter. At least we've got some nice sunshine today.

Trav let his wine rest under his tongue, savoring the taste. "Nice wine."

"Yes. It's not bad."

John Reighspier, Spear to his friends, had lost Mrs. Reighspier to cancer the previous winter. It had been a long, tough siege. The frontal assaults with radiation and chemotherapy had forced the "Big C" to retreat, to go dormant and then regroup. The cancer lost many battles, but it was a war of attrition and the cancer won the final battle. After his wife's death, Spear promised himself he would continue his private practice as a psychiatrist. And he kept the promise for almost a year. But by summer's end, the counseling sessions had become dry and rote, he had told Trav. He would end his profession of thirty years and write. Yes, that would be it. The novel that was still and forever in his head, the one about the war, his war, Korea, his love and the heart's journey.

Trav stared into the yellow-orange flames of the fire before him. "How's the book coming, Spear?"

"The book? Yes, indeed. It's still up here, I'm afraid," Spear said, placing a forefinger to his temple.

Trav turned to face his friend. "Labor Day it was. Labor Day weekend you told me you were closing up the practice so you could write.

"I did."

"You did what?"

"I did tell you that."

"And?"

"And I'm finding it very hard. Hard to start."

They sipped in silence, sitting side by side, looking into the flames.

"What do you hear from Daniel?" Spear asked finally.

"Oh," Trav started, a hint of resignation in his voice. "He and his counselor call us once a week. He's doing okay, I guess. Just not sure."

"Well, you've done everything you could," Spear said, "You can't save him from himself. It's up to him now."

Trav sighed, stroking the stem of his wine glass with his thumb and forefinger. "I just wish I could have a normal father-son relationship with that kid."

"Well, let me tell you, my friend," said Spear, "those normal relations, whatever the hell normal is, are pretty few and far between."

"Yeah, I suppose."

Spear stood, walked into the kitchen and stirred the stew. Shuffling back into the den, he asked, "You and your dad have a normal father-son relationship?"

Trav, caught with wine in his mouth, coughed and gagged. Regaining control, he looked up at Spear and snorted, "Are you kidding?"

After some gentle prodding coupled with a refill of wine, Trav started to talk about his growing up days in a small town just west of Charlotte, North Carolina. He told Spear about his father's roughness, his distance from him and his drinking. The conversation pulled Trav into a patchy reverie. Imperfect memories of days and nights almost a half century ago.

"My mother said I almost died the day I was born. Lost oxygen in the womb. Came out not breathing. I guess I spent a long time in the hospital," Trav said.

The afternoon light softened the view from the den window. It was past time to eat, but Trav was still talking and Spear made no move to interrupt him. Trav circled back to the subject of his father.

"Get this," Trav said, "A year before I was born, my grandmother—my father's mother—committed suicide. Hung herself in a closet."

"Wow," said Spear. "You never told me. That's extraordinary."

"Not really. Lots of people off themselves. What *is* extraordinary is that my father never uttered one word to me about it. Not one. I was forty-five when he died."

"How did you even know?"

"My mother told me when I was college-age."

Spear glanced at his friend. "Pal, we've known each other for fifteen years and you never told me this."

Trav looked over at Spear, belatedly realizing the irony. "That's different, Spear." he snapped. "We're neighbors, not father and son."

"I was simply..."

"Can you imagine? Forty-five years? Not one word."

Spear reached for the two glasses, rose quietly and padded again into the kitchen, this time to turn off the heat under the stew. He called over his shoulder, "Tell me more about your father."

"Like what more?"

"Just tell. Who was he?"

Trav absently reached for his wine glass, not realizing Spear had taken it away. He took a deep breath.

"My father was born in Atlanta during World War One. There were five children. He put himself through college. Studied chemistry. Got a job that made dynamite and later, munitions for the military. They wouldn't let him join up for World War II because he had to stay and make the ammo. He stayed with that same company until he retired."

Spear came back into the den and sat down. "Who was he for you, Trav?"

"What do you mean? He was my father."

Spear repeated, "Who was he for you?"

*Psychiatrists ask bizarre questions*, Trav thought. He looked again into the flames, seemingly mesmerized by the dancing veils of yellow and orange. Then he began to feel the question. Something in his chest stirred. Slowly, haltingly at first, words stumbled from his lips, then began to pour full and open.

"He was gone a lot. An awful lot. A week or two at a time. I still have a stack of post cards, maybe fifty, he mailed to me from his trips. I really loved him, looked up to him. But you know—and I never saw this as a kid—but thinking back on it now, even when he was home, he wasn't really home. He'd get up early and go to work. Played golf on Saturdays, then come home and watch golf on the TV with his scotch and water."

Trav tapped his fingers against one another. "I played varsity basketball in high school, junior and senior year. Do you know my parents *never* came to watch me? They weren't bad parents. Not bad people. I think maybe they just thought sports were part of school. It didn't occur to them to sit in on a math class. Why would they go to a basketball game?"

Spear asked, "But it hurt didn't it?"

"Yeah, it hurt. It still hurts," Trav said, his voice just above a whisper. Then he added, "I promised myself a long time ago that I would be a different kind of father to my children, to my son."

Trav sat motionless. The quiet, hypnotizing dance of flames pulled him further back into his painful childhood.

Finally, Spear coughed and made a shuffling noise with his feet. "Ready to eat?"

"Sure," Trav said, still looking into the fire. "Ready."

# CHAPTER 6

## The Phone Call

The phone was ringing. *What the hell?* Martha rolled over in the bed and sat up. "What time is it?"

Trav looked at the clock on the bureau. Five minutes past six. He reached for the phone. "Hello."

"Mister McGale?"

"Yes?"

"This is Dan O'Malley. I'm sorry to be calling so early."

Trav tightened his grip on the phone. "That's alright."

Martha was now sitting on the edge of the bed. "Who is it?"

Trav cupped his hand over the speaker and turned his head. "It's the school." He turned back into O'Malley's voice. "...and we needed to let you know right away. Daniel and two other boys are not on campus. We presume they ran away in the middle of the night."

Trav groaned, "Oh, Christ!"

"What?" Martha asked.

"Daniel's run away. Go pick up downstairs."

Martha bolted out of the bedroom as O'Malley continued.

"I know this is worrisome. Would be for any parent, but I would ask you not to overreact. Almost every year we have runaways. Sometimes several. In ninety percent of the cases, the students return on their own within two or three days. We have already notified the authorities here in town. Standard procedure."

Martha was on the line in the kitchen. "Where would he go?"

27

"There's no way of knowing for sure," O'Malley said, " but typically these kids hitchhike into Brewenton, find an all-night diner or a bus or train depot and hang out for a while."

"And then what?" Trav asked.

O'Malley chose not to address Trav's "then what." Instead, he said, "Some of the boys' clothes and personal items are missing and their back packs are not here. That suggests they planned this ahead of time. I would like to suggest to both of you that you adopt an attitude...and you can help support each other here... of not enabling, not running after Daniel." O'Malley paused, waiting for either Trav or Martha to respond, but there was no response. He continued quietly, "There are times in life when the best thing to do is do nothing. For the two of you, this is one of those times."

Martha asked, "Have Burson-Mann runaways always come back?"

"Not always," the headmaster said, "but it is quite uncommon that they don't. I wanted you to know what has happened as soon as we knew. We have all of your numbers: cell, home, office. We'll call immediately if we have news."

Trav, his voice flat, said, "Okay, Dan. We'll wait to hear."

"I hope you both are involved in Al Anon," O'Malley said. "It will help you both."

Martha managed a weak, "Good-bye."

Trav hung up the bedroom phone and went down to the kitchen. Martha had both palms out flat on the granite counter, head bent down, her brown hair falling forward over her ears, still as a statue. He quietly drew close behind and put his arms around her waist. He nestled his face in her hair. He felt her take a deep, long breath.

"It never ends with that boy, does it?" he whispered. He released his embrace and rested his hip on the kitchen counter. Martha, simply out of morning habit, walked toward the coffee maker and reached up into the cabinet over the sink for a paper filter.

"So," asked Trav, "we do what O'Malley suggests? We do nothing?"

"No," Martha said, "we don't do nothing. We keep going to the Al Anon meetings like the school suggested and we pray to God for grace and for help. And we pray that God will be with our son." She began filling the glass coffee pot with water from the faucet. "And we pray for wisdom to do the right thing."

The right thing, thought Trav, is to get in the car, drive to Maine and find the damn kid. But Trav did not drive to Maine. He also did not do nothing. He didn't pray as Martha had suggested, but he went about his Saturday morning routine. Later, Martha went off to her ladies club wreath-making event. Trav sat at his home desk puttering with bills and correspondence. He worried and layered his worry with more worry. Martha worried also but overlaid her worry with prayer and supplication.

# CHAPTER 7

## Al Anon

It was their third meeting. Trav looked around the room, counting those present. It was an old habit of his begun who knows when, who knows where. At the law firm staff meetings, years earlier at father-son Cub Scout events, and today in the basement of All Saints Catholic Church, his eyes scanned the circle of folding chairs. He always counted the people present. Tonight, there were seventeen, including himself and Martha. Ten women, seven men. A woman with a large blue and white scarf around her neck read from a three-ring binder on her lap, "We welcome you to the Parents' Thursday Al Anon meeting and hope you will find in this fellowship the help and friendship we have been privileged to enjoy. We who have lived with the problems of drugs and alcohol understand as perhaps few others can. We urge you to try our program."

Trav's mind wandered back to their first day at the school in Maine. Trav remembered Dan O'Malley strongly advising Trav and Martha to join Al Anon and repeating the recommendation during the painful early morning telephone call.

The lady with the blue and white scarf was still speaking. "I'm Janice, a grateful member of Al Anon and I thought I would lead tonight with today's reading from *Courage to Change*."

Janice read a short passage from a small book with a mustard yellow cover, then proceeded to talk about her nineteen-year-old daughter who was a heroin addict, had gone to New York City the

31

previous spring, but was now in a drug rehabilitation facility in Virginia. Trav could tell that Martha was listening intently. He tried to listen too, but soon was swept into a silent conversation with himself. Someone deep in the recesses of his craw had once again pressed the 'play' button.

And so it began. *Where the hell was he? By himself? With those two other boys? No. O'Malley had called after three days to report that the two boys had come back to the school. Why won't Daniel answer his cell phone? Maybe he doesn't have his charger. Shit. Maybe I should...*

Martha, crossing her legs, bumped Trav's ankle and brought him back to the meeting.

Janice was wrapping up, "....and so I don't know what's going to happen with Joy. She's in a good place now with good help. But it's up to her. She has to want a different life. I'll be honest. I'm scared. But at least she's not on the streets in New York City doing God knows what. I just know I'm glad to be here. That's it, I guess. Thank you for listening."

After the other sixteen in the room said in unison, "Thank you for sharing," there ensued an hour of sharing and discussion. Trav shifted and re-shifted his position on the metal folding chair. He tried to pay attention to the shares, but his mind kept wandering.

At precisely seven p.m., Janice brought the meeting to its close. "Talk to each other, reason things out with someone else. Now, will all who care to join us in the Serenity Prayer."

Trav and Martha stood along with the others, stepping forward and joining hands in a circle of anxious parents. They closed their eyes, all except Trav, and began, "God, grant me the serenity to accept the things I cannot change, the courage to change the things I can and the wisdom to know the difference."

The group pumped their still joined hands up and down and said together, "Keep coming back. It works if you work it."

They walked out of the church basement into a cloudless December night. The pale whiteness of the far distant stars accentuated the cold. *How cold the night air was in Maine. Was Daniel out in it tonight? Freezing? Hands numb?* He opened the passenger side door for Martha and moved quickly around to the driver's side. He started the engine as Martha complained, "Oh God, it's cold!" She turned the heater knob on full, only to feel a blast of frigid air on her bare legs.

Trav turned the dial back to off. "Hang on. It's gotta warm up for a minute."

Martha rubbed her mittened hands together. "Brrrrrrrr."

They drove in silence for a few minutes. Few other cars were out on this frigid night. They passed a large dark bundle on a heated sidewalk grate. Trav studied it as they passed. A homeless person, he was sure, was under the pile of blankets. *Maybe a teenager? Maybe a drug addict?*

Martha could wait no longer and once again turned the on the heater. This time, blessed warm air flowed out and on to her legs. She glanced over to her husband. "Good meeting, don't you think?"

Trav sighed and replied without enthusiasm. "Yeah. I guess."

"What was the matter with it?" Martha asked.

"Oh, I don't know. I just..." Trav's thought, whatever it was, slipped away.

"What?"

"Well, I just..." He hesitated, then started again. "There's something about that Serenity Prayer we all say each time that kind of bothers me."

"What bothers you?"

"The serenity to accept the things I cannot change. That stuff. It's like we just have to sit around and be powerless. Do nothing. It's not how I was raised to live my life."

Martha looked over at him again and said, "Don't forget the other part. 'The courage to change the things I can.' That's not powerless."

Trav, now with more energy in his voice, said, "I just feel like those folks in there think we should do nothing about Daniel."

Martha took her gloves off and reached her palms into the warm air. "Well, maybe they're right." She looked over at him. "What would you do?"

"Well, for one thing, "Trav said, "I would take this car and drive to Maine and get him."

Martha thought about that for a moment, then said, "That's right. You could drive to Maine. You are not powerless over that. But I think the point of the program is that we are powerless over Daniel. We are powerless over his addiction, over his attitude, over his decisions. All of it."

The traffic light in front of them turned from red to green. Trav accelerated with a touch of angry energy, saying, "Well, I don't know. It's just not the way I was raised. It's not the way to get things done in life."

Martha was struggling to stay calm. "I think the problem is you're trying to get things done in someone else's life, not yours," she said.

# CHAPTER 8

## *Christmas*

It was the shortest day of the year, the winter solstice. Trav was on his hands and knees positioning the Christmas tree trunk into the stand. Pine needles from the lowest branch scratched the back of his neck. *God, the kids aren't little anymore. Why can't we get a small artificial tree? Yes, Martha says every year, maybe next year. But next year the artificial Christmas tree always gets rescheduled for one more year.*

A protruding branch pricked him behind the ear.

"Ow! Goddammit!."

Martha was standing, cantilevered forward, straddling her husband's derriere, holding the top of the tree.

"Please don't use that language, especially at Christmas."

Trav, grunting and struggling to align the sappy tree trunk in the stand, muttered from below, "Sure dear. Just give me an approved list of seasonally-appropriate expletives."

"Oh, come on, Trav. Don't."

"Will you...wait a sec...okay, now. Push the top so it's straight up and down."

Just then the front door opened. "Hello?"

Martha, holding the tree with both hands, called over her shoulder, "Eryn, is that you?"

"Merry Christmas!"

Martha instinctively started to turn, taking a step backward.

A frustrated voice grunted from below, "Don't let go of the tree, dammit!"

Martha refocused on the task at hand and pushed the leaning spruce back to vertical while calling into the front hall, "In here, honey. I thought you said tonight, eight or nine."

"They cancelled the last classes," Eryn said, turning into the living room. "Hi. Where's Dad?"

"Oh, I put him away for the season. You know he doesn't like Christmas." Martha said with an airy, cheerful tone.

"Ho. Ho. Ho," came a voice from under the tree. Eryn spotted two shoe soles and a dungareed rear-end between her mother's legs.

"Hey, Dad."

⚜

Trav was happy to have their daughter home. Her usual buoyancy helped lift his own spirits. That evening, he, Martha and Eryn were at the small table in the family room. It was a cozy winter meal of lamb chops, Martha's home-made corn bread and salad. Trav had once again put on the *Corelli's Mandolin* music.

"You know, we do have a few other tapes. I think Mr. Corelli must be exhausted," Martha said.

"I like it," Trav said, bending his head to capture a mouthful of stew.

"I like it too," said Eryn, playing out a long-established gravitational pull toward her father.

Trav glanced at Eryn, enjoying the sight of her hair, now twisted on top of her head, and her bright open face.

"So, how's school?" asked Martha.

"It's good. No complaints," Eryn said in a tone of muted enthusiasm. "Classes going okay. We had a cool end of season soccer party. Really fun."

They ate without speaking for a long minute. Finally, with an air of forced nonchalance, Eryn asked, "Any word from Daniel?"

It was an abrupt, startling shift in emotional gears for which neither Trav nor Martha was fully prepared.

"No," said Trav. "Nothing. He doesn't answer calls or texts to his cell. The school is keeping us posted, but their posts are always 'no news.'"

Eryn said, "It's been almost two weeks."

"Yes, Eryn," Trav snapped. "We know it's been almost two weeks."

Martha glared at her husband. "Get a grip."

They ate again in silence. Folks and knives scraped uneasily on plates.

Finally, Martha spoke. "It's been a rough ride with Daniel. For all of us. The acting out, the defiance, the temper tantrums. The different schools. When he was little, I tried so hard, calling other mothers to get their boys to come and play. They came and played, but usually only once. We did testing, counseling, meds for ADD, ADHD, mood swings. He's smart, so smart. But the performance and the behavior..." Her voice trailed off.

Trav took an ample swallow of merlot. "He's been a challenge for seventeen years. He came into this world with two strikes against him. Full term. Low birth weight. Intestines messed up. Fetal alcohol syndrome. At least that's what the agency told us."

Eryn had stopped eating. Her hands, straddling her plate, were balled into tight fists.

Trav sipped more wine and then continued. "Tough start. And when we adopted him..."

"When you adopted Daniel?" Eryn interrupted hotly, her lips quivering with anger. "When you adopted Daniel? This house anymore is nothing but Daniel, Daniel, Daniel. That's all I hear when I come home."

"Eryn, you were the one who just asked us about him," Trav said.

Martha leaned in toward her daughter. "Honey, please..."

"Shut up, Mom! This has been boiling in me for a long time now and I'm going to say it! Yes, I asked. He's my brother and I'm sorry Daniel has been a problem for you. I'm sorry he got into drugs and drinking. I'm sorry you had to send him to Maine and I'm sorry he's run away. Yeah, you guys adopted him."

Then Eryn stopped and turned to face her father with a withering intensity.

"I happen to be adopted too, you know. Maybe you forgot. I've had my own problems and heartaches. But you never talk about me. I'm the good kid. I got good grades. I stayed out of trouble. I'm in college. And what's my reward? I get ignored! It's all Daniel, Daniel, Daniel! I'm sick of it!"

Eryn put her face in her hands and sobbed. "This family is so fucked up!"

Martha put her fork on her plate and closed her eyes. Trav quietly reached over and put his hand on Eryn's shoulder. She recoiled.

"Don't touch me!"

She stood, knocking her chair over and ran out of the room. They heard her running footsteps on the stairs and then heard her bedroom door slam. Martha stood, picked up her plate and glass and went into the kitchen. Trav thought he heard them both crying.

He sat stunned, motionless, staring at the space of emptiness before him. From his seat in the dining room, he could see their Christmas tree now adorned with strands of white lights.

*How can that tree just stand there so still, so peaceful, amidst a family where two are in tears, one is missing and the fourth, now gazing at the tree, feels an engulfing sadness?*

He turned away from the living room and did what he so often did when he didn't know what else to do. He poured himself another glass of wine, retreated to The Room of the Flying Chair and turned down the volume on his favorite music. He sipped of the ruby red elixir and closed his eyes, letting the sadness and fear wash through him. Another, larger "sip." Corelli's music played through and was starting again at the beginning.

# CHAPTER 9

## The Decision

February. *Thank God there are only twenty-eight days in this miserable month.* A few inches of crusted snow covered the loop path. Through the maze of leafless branches, the back door light of Spear's house came into view. Trav veered off the path, cutting through the narrow tree line toward his friend's house. The back door, as usual, was slightly ajar.

They settled once again in the big armchairs. Trav extended his arms, palms out, to capture the warmth of the fire.

"Gad, its cold out there!"

"It is that," Spear said. "Toughest winter I can remember." He reached to the coffee table for a Ritz cracker and a square of Swiss cheese. "So how are you and Martha holding up?"

Trav shrugged. "Okay, I guess. It's hard, though. I wake up in the middle of the night wondering where he is, what he's doing, is he alright?"

"What does the school say?"

"What they've always said. 'Just hold tight. Don't rescue. Don't enable.'"

Spear chewed on his cheese and cracker, then asked, "Are those Al Anon meetings good? They helpful to you?"

Trav didn't want to answer the question because he knew he would be chided. *What the hell.*

"Actually," he said, deciding on honesty, "I've stopped going. I went to three meetings. Martha still goes."

Spear looked over at his friend.

"Three, huh? That seems to be the magic number for you. You lasted three sessions with the VA counselor. Three Al Anon meetings." Spear, a small, sly grin on his face, added, "I'm detecting a pattern here."

Trav couldn't disagree.

"Yeah, I know. I just didn't feel real comfortable....."

Spear broke in. "Ol' buddy, the meetings, the counseling are not there to make you comfortable. They are there to provide insight and support. Growth. Healing."

Trav sighed.

"I know. I know."

The fire hissed and crackled.

Spear bit his upper lip, scratched his nose and then said, "I know you know. You know, but you don't do."

Trav said nothing. Spear changed the subject.

"You told me before a little about the day you were born. The medical problems. Rushed to an incubator. Stayed there for quite a while, I'm guessing."

"I suppose," Trav mused.

"Probably didn't get held much by your mama."

"I expect not. How could she if I was in one of those contraptions?"

Spear, trying to remember that he was talking to a friend, not a patient, thought about what he might say next.

Looking straight ahead into the fireplace, he said, "You know, you might want to write to the hospital where you were born. Ask them to send you any reports on your birth."

Trav looked over at his friend. "Why?"

"Oh, I don't know," Spear said. "It might be interesting. As a general rule, I think the more we all know about ourselves, the better off we are."

Trav mulled Spear's suggestion over for a minute.

"Maybe I will."

Spear changed the subject again.

"So you don't hear anything at all from Daniel?"

Trav took a deep breath and exhaled slowly.

"Well, bits and pieces. Someone who works at the school thought they saw him crossing the street in Brewenton. Two weeks ago, I sent him a text asking if he was alright. The next day he answered, 'I'm OK.'" Then yesterday, I sent another text. 'Are you really OK?'" He responded right away. 'Sort of.' Then I asked by text what that meant. No answer."

Trav reached for his drink.

"This is driving me crazy. I mean really crazy. The school keeps telling us to leave him alone. Martha says the same. I know she's as worried as I am, but she's bought into all this detach with love stuff. Don't enable. Let him lead his life. He has to figure things out." Trav drank his wine. "Shit! I just hate this."

Spear stood to poke the burning logs. With his back to Trav, he spoke into the fireplace.

"Maybe they're right."

"Right?" challenged Trav angrily. "And maybe Daniel has gone in with a drug gang. And maybe he'll get knifed or shot or die from an overdose. Whose right, then, Dr. Shrink? If you were me and you sat around drinking by a nice warm fire while your son dies and you did nothing to try and stop it, could you live with yourself? Would you just sit and sip cabernet and accept that risk?"

Spear said nothing.

Trav pushed on.

"Well, would you?"

Spear answered, "I'm not in your shoes. If I were, I'd be torn six ways from Sunday. I know I would. But we don't live in a risk-free world. We don't live in a world without danger and we don't live in a world without suffering."

Trav interjected, "And we also don't live in a world where people are rewarded for doing nothing."

Spear shifted the conversation.

"How old is Daniel now?"

"Seventeen. He'll be eighteen March 15."

"Ah," Spear chuckled. "Beware the Ides of March."

"Beware is right. He becomes a legal adult in a little more than a month."

"You know, you just might be underestimating Daniel. He's a smart kid. You've told me that."

"Yeah. He's smart up here," Trav said, putting a finger to his forehead. "But he's an emotional mess. He flies off the handle all the time and he makes bad decisions."

"Well, I just think maybe you don't give him enough credit."

"Credit?" Trav was incredulous. "Credit? He's ruining his life and he's turned our family into turmoil!"

"I would just suggest that you..."

Trav's face reddened. He turned toward Spear. He looked at his friend for a long moment and then said, "You're on their side, aren't you? You think I should do nothing."

Spear tried to calm his friend.

"Look, I don't know what the right answer is. I really don't. And this isn't majority rule."

"You're damn right it isn't!" Trav spat. "That's my son up there in some goddamned ghetto and I care about him and I have a responsibility as a father to...." He stopped suddenly. Spear looked over and saw a glistening in his eyes.

"Trav," he said softly, putting his hand on his friend's forearm. "This is hard. Real hard. You're a good man."

Trav wiped his eyes with his sleeve and stared into the embers of the dying fire. Then, in a voice barely above a whisper, he said, "I'm going to go get him."

# CHAPTER 10

## The Drive North

Even after an hour of driving, the coffee in the plastic travel mug was still hot. Trav reached for the mug and put the lid to his lips. The interstate north was fast, but the scenery was repetitive and the drive was boring. He turned the radio on, scanned for pleasing music or some news that was actually new. He clicked the radio off, then a minute later, on again. Then once more off. He took another long swallow of coffee, accelerated to seventy miles per hour and then hit the cruise button.

For the second or maybe third time since leaving the house at dawn, he replayed in his mind his conversation with Martha the night before. They were having dinner at home. Martha was telling him something about her sister and her sister's husband's business. Trav was not listening. He was thinking about his conversation with Spear the previous afternoon and he was thinking and worrying about Daniel. Martha interrupted her own monologue and looked over.

"Are you listening?"

Trav chewed, then swallowed and said with uncharacteristic candor, "I'm sorry. No, I'm not. I'm really not. I'm just..."

"You're sitting there thinking about Daniel, aren't you?"

"Yes, I am!" he said boldly. "Of course I am! Aren't you? Don't tell me you're not worried too. Come on. I see that look on your face sometimes. I know you're up in the middle of the night. Be honest."

"Of course I'm worried," said Martha. "But I just can't do anything about it. We can't and worrying doesn't help anything."

Trav reached for his drink, saying at the same time, "Worrying doesn't do anything, but..." He stopped, then started again. "Spear and I talked yesterday. We talked about the situation, about Daniel and..."

Martha arched her eyebrows.

"And?"

"And I think the situation is getting out of hand. It's been six weeks now. Six weeks! The kid is wandering around the State of Maine in the middle of winter. He has no money unless he stole it. Where is he staying? How does he eat? Stay warm? I just don't think we're being responsible parents."

Martha looked at her husband, her irritation turning toward empathy. She reached out to put a comforting hand on his. He pulled away.

"You know," he said, turning toward Martha. "think about it. I mean, really take a step back and look into this house. A loving man and woman have a seventeen-year-old son. He's got emotional issues. He may be bipolar. Who knows? He's hundreds of miles away from home, middle of winter. He runs away from a special school. And what do these loving parents do?" He looked hard into Martha's eyes. "What do they do, Martha? Nothing. Zip. Nada. Not a goddamned thing!"

"Trav, please, I know..."

He cut her off.

"I'm telling you, Martha. This isn't right. I'm not going to just sit here one more day, one more night. I'm not!"

"Please," said Martha. "Can we talk? Can we be calm and talk?"

"We've been talking, haven't we, for six weeks. And talking to the school. And by the way, if I have to listen to that goddamned headmaster tell me one more time to 'let go of outcomes' and to 'focus on myself,' I'm going to kill him with my bare hands!"

From her quarter of a century of marriage to this man, Martha knew the character and path of the storm. Hurricane Traveler would start slowly, then build and build. She also knew not to get in its direct path. The tempest's internal energies had to run their course and dissipate at their own pace and of their own accord. And so she simply sat and listened and waited. He cooled slightly and the gale slowed.

As the storm abated, he continued, "I just can't do nothing. I can't. I'm going up there. I'm going to find him."

They had talked about this before. Martha was against the idea and Trav was keenly aware of her opposition. But Martha also knew there was no use arguing any more.

৩৯৬৯

The honking of a passing truck on his left brought Trav back to the road and to his path north. He was driving to Maine to find his son. He had his goal, but he didn't really have a plan. Would he go to the school? Would he tell O'Malley he had come to find Daniel? Would he contact the police? Maybe he should text Daniel. Yes? No? Would that push him deeper into hiding? And another question, not a trivial one, rose to the fore: If he did find Daniel, what would he say to him? I want you to go back to the school? I want you to come home with me? Trav thought of the old joke about the dog that each morning ran barking after the garbage truck. What would the dog do if he caught it? Like the dog, he was pushed on—not by a plan—but by instinct and emotion.

He stopped for gas and more coffee. Coming out of the Quik Stop with a hot lidded coffee, he walked to his silver Honda. He put his coffee on the car roof, turned to the pump register, topped off until the price showed an even thirty-three dollars. He hated receipts that were not even to the dollar. He twisted the gas tank cap tight and closed the little door. As he pressed 'yes' for receipt, he glanced over at the car next to him. It was a station wagon, an old one with the real wood paneling on the sides. A boy, five years old, maybe six, was sitting in the passenger side looking at Trav. The boy's father—Trav was sure it was his father—was pumping gas. Trav turned back to retrieve his receipt, then opened the driver's side door to his own car. He looked again at the station wagon. It was the same car his father had. Same color, same wooden side paneling. He looked at the boy who was still staring at him. Trav waved to him. The boy, seeming puzzled, looked away.

45

He got in his car, started the engine, pulled out of the gas station and eased back onto the interstate. As he accelerated into the flow of the traffic, he glanced down at his empty mug. *Shit!* He had forgotten his fresh coffee that was surely no longer on the car roof. Without fresh coffee to comfort him, Trav again fidgeted with the radio. Country music, then to an all-news station, then to light rock. Nothing satisfied. He switched the radio off and took a long, bored gaze at the passing Pennsylvania forests and even less interesting media strip flowing by on his left. A pale yellow sun was now rising over the treeline to his right.

He couldn't get that little kid out of his mind. *What was it?* Maybe it was the old station wagon and that wood paneling. Real wood. What a classic. In an instant, the scene came to him. They were on vacation in Nags Head, North Carolina. Trav was five, maybe six. They were all together, his twin sister, Trav, and his mother and father. Every summer, they went to the same motel and to the same beach near Oregon Inlet. Not many people went to that stretch of shoreline. The sand was hard enough that Trav's father could drive the old woody right onto to the beach. They didn't have to carry the beach chairs, the umbrella, the cooler full of beer, the toys and Dad's fishing gear. It would all be there in the car next to them.

It was a cloudless July day with a light offshore breeze. Little Trav, plastic pail in hand, was ankle deep in the gentle surf. He was building a wet sandcastle midway between the surf and the family encampment. The boy looked back at the three of them sitting in their rickety aluminum chairs. Recalling now that day so long ago, grown Trav sensed that there was another boy, a second boy, there with them. Strange. *What was that all about?*

Young Trav called. "Dad!" No response.

"Dad, come help me."

Samuel McGale was opening his second bottle of cold beer. He never drank during the day, except when he was on vacation. Maybe on Saturdays...and on holidays. Also when there was a football game on television. But other than those times, hardly ever.

"Dad!"

The father turned and looked expressionlessly at his son.

"In a bit."

Young Trav never could fathom how long 'a bit' was. With his father, it was usually a long time. He could see his mother turn to his father and say something, but with the noise of the waves behind him, he couldn't make out what she was saying. It seemed like some kind of argument. He watched his father take a long pull on his beer, then walk to the rear of the old woody to retrieve his surf casting rod. Trav resumed work alone on his sandcastle.

Down the beach, his father stood thigh-deep in the Atlantic surf. The boy regarded his father. In less than a week on vacation, he already had a masculine, swarthy tan. His face, with a two-day growth and dark glasses, was shadowed under his floppy, khaki fisherman's hat. The man slowly rotated the long pole back behind him. He looked forward out to sea. Then, with a fluid, sweeping arc, he flung the weighted bait and hooks out beyond the surf line. The boy tried to follow the tackle on its flight, but lost sight of it until he saw the white splash far out beyond the breaking waves.

Trav loved his father. He loved him in spite of the anger and the drinking and the distance between them. He wanted to go over there and help hold the fishing pole. He waved a young boy's 'hi,' but his father's gaze was intent on the vastness of the ocean before him and the catch he was sure was moving out there below the surface.

Grown Trav drove through the morning out of Pennsylvania and into New York State. It seemed silly to him, but he couldn't resist the urge to look in the rearview mirror for the old woody which, as it turned out, was nowhere to be seen. The ever-present voice in his head began to chatter away. *Is this trip a mistake? Maybe I should have deferred to Martha's sense.* Spear had counseled him: "Look to your intention and to your angst. If you think about it," he had said, "every human action, every one, is motivated either by fear or love."

Ramos and Spear must have studied together. Trav remembered their talk well. All too well. That particular Sunday afternoon, the old psychiatrist had stood and poured some more cabernet into Trav's glass and sat back down.

"So," he had said, "you're going to drive to Maine by yourself. Martha's not going. And you're going up there to search for your son who, by the way, has given no indication that he wants to be found, right?"

Trav nodded.

"Right."

"But you are bound and determined, aren't you?" Spear paused. "Driven to drive, I would say."

"Yes, doc," said Trav, irritated. "I can't disagree."

"Of course you can't," said Spear. "But the real question is why. Why are you so locked in on this?"

Trav thought for a minute, trying to formulate the 'right' answer to his doctor friend.

"Well, I think it's just that..."

Spear cut him off.

"Let me give you a hint. The answer has almost nothing to do with what you are thinking."

"What?"

"I just told you a minute ago. Fear and love. It's all fear and love." The ever-present burning logs in the fireplace crackled and sputtered and hissed. Spear continued, now in a gentler, almost fatherly tone. "Trav, I am not saying you shouldn't go up there. Maybe it's a good thing to do. I'm only saying it will help you—and Daniel and Martha—to know, to really know why you are going."

Trav was feeling agitated and on the defensive.

"Alright, Doctor Shrink, you're the expert here apparently. Why am I going?"

Spear held his gaze for a long moment.

"What do you love?"

Trav squirmed and then shrugged.

"I love all kinds of things and people and places."

Spear wasn't going to let him get off with that answer.

"Yes, I know. But we're talking here about a solo trip up to northern New England." Spear waited, then asked again, "What do you love?"

Trav closed his eyes and put one hand to his cheek.

"I love my son," he said quietly.

"Right," Spear whispered. "You love your son. And what are you afraid of?"

Trav opened his eyes, looked over at Spear, then straight ahead into the fire.

"I'm afraid I'm going to lose him. I'm afraid something really bad might..." He stopped.

Spear picked up the theme and said in a hushed voice, "Yeah, something bad. Or maybe that Daniel up there in Maine somewhere might decide that he simply doesn't want to be with his father."

Trav winced.

"Yeah, that too. That's a different kind of something bad, but either way..." He stopped again.

"Yes," said Spear. "Either way. You love your son and you're afraid you're going to lose him and you want to go rescue him."

Trav began to cry. Through his tears, he muffled out, "Bingo. That's it exactly."

Spear stood, walked behind his friend and put his hands on his shoulders. "If you go..."

Trav interrupted him.

"You still think the trip is a bad idea, don't you?

Spear took in a long deep breath, then breathed out through his nostrils.

"You know, I have my thoughts. But I'm not you and Daniel's not my son. But I can tell you this. If you do go, you will know clearly now *why* you are going. And that's a good thing."

&#x6723;&#x6729;

After his driving-while-daydreaming return to Spear's pine paneled den, he forced himself to think hard about what he would actually do once he got to Maine. He even retrieved a three-by-five card from his breast pocket, positioned it flat against the hub of the steering wheel and, while rocketing north at seventy-five miles an hour, made notes to himself. He wrote : *1) See O'M*. Yes, for sure, in the morning he would go to the school and visit with the headmaster. Then next he would—he would—well, it would depend on what O'Malley had to say. So his 'plan' worked out over an hour and outlined in detail on his three-by-five card read:

*Step One. Visit Dan O'Malley*

*Step Two. Figure out next steps after completing Step One.*

It was almost ten at night when Trav approached the outskirts of Pender Bay, Maine. An hour's drive north of Brewenton, Pender Bay lay on the south coast of a long, finger-like peninsula. A small town that late on a hard winter night appeared frozen in deep hibernation. The streets and sidewalks were devoid of sentient beings. The center village traffic light blinked yellow in the frigid air. Trav turned left at the light, vaguely remembering a motel at the top of the hill.

The night clerk checked him into a sparse but clean room. Two twin beds, a night table between the beds, a television and a larger wooden table with uneven, wobbly legs.

Climbing into bed, he laid his cell phone on the night table and looked at the small screen. Maybe he should call Martha. He had hope she would call, but he knew she was opposed to the trip. Maybe she would still call to see if he had arrived safely. He left the phone on in case, thinking more that Daniel just might call or text. He was very tired from the drive and he was mentally fatigued from his struggle to come up with anything that resembled a meaningful course of action.

He reached for the lamp next to the bed and clicked the room into darkness. An hour later, he was still awake and he knew why. At home, it was the same. When he left his cell phone on, he was, consciously or not, 'on watch' for that possible incoming call or text. So he would lay in bed, his body at rest, his mind on quiet alert and sleep would not come. Finally, at midnight, he rolled toward the night table, reached for the cell phone and powered off.

☙❧

Sleep came at last and so did the dream. It was the same, always the same. A misty rain had turned the low hill into a slippery, coffee-colored mud. Vince was ten meters or so ahead of him. In the dim, early morning light, he could only make out his friend's helmet and the drab camouflage of his jungle fatigues. The area, once a thick jungle, had been denuded by Agent Orange and repetitive air strikes. A battalion of North Vietnamese regulars were pressing in on their outpost. First came the low distant thrumph of bombing, then the rat-tat-tat of incoming and outgoing machine gun fire.

Decades ago, in an all too wakened state, Trav had heard Vince cry out in agony, "God...oh God...oh God!" And he had rushed—in a low, crawling duck walk—forward to the side of his best friend, the true brother he never had, fellow Marine Vincent Lanzinito. The dying Marine was on his stomach, head twisted grotesquely to one side. Trav turned his friend's head to see his full face, but there was no full face to see.

In the dream, it happened a different way. He slipped again and again on the slippery mud. He gained no traction and repeatedly reached an outstretched hand into the night rain. Lanzi kept screaming while Trav kept failing to move forward. Trav cried out in the dream as he had, in fact, that night on the other side of the world, "Don't die on me, you son of a bitch! Don't leave me alone!" Trav laid his head on Lanzi's back and moaned, "No, no, no." He lay still for a minute, as still and almost as lifeless as his friend. Then he clenched his rifle and shouted at the top of his lungs, "Medic! Medic!"

He woke with the wetness of perspiration on his neck and pillow. For a moment, he was lost. *Where am I?* A pale dawn light seeped around the blinds of the motel window. He raised himself on one elbow and surveyed his surroundings. *Oh, yes. Maine. Right.* He shaved, showered and dressed, then returned to the single bed and sat on the edge by the night table. He turned on his cell phone and stared at the small screen, waiting for the beep announcing a new message. He stared for a full minute. No message.

# CHAPTER 11

## *The Search*

Trav stepped out into the Maine winter morning. It was snowing. He had forgotten his gloves and his ice scraper was at home in the trunk of their other car. With his bare hand, he brushed the powdery snow off the front windshield and opened the car door. But he did not step in. Instead, with one hand on the rim of the open door, he looked up through incoming snowflakes to the towering dark pines that surrounded the motel. It was a soft, deep quiet, the kind that only comes with a windless snow. Trav closed his eyes. *That dream. That damn dream. How many times?*

It had been less than three months since he and Martha and Daniel had first climbed the stone steps leading to the Bacon-Mann administration building, but it seemed like a lifetime ago. The steps had been shoveled that morning, but were already covered again with the new snow that was blanketing all of New England. In the foyer of the converted Victorian home, the receptionist looked up from her computer.

"Good morning."

"Good morning. Hi. Is Dan O'Malley in?"

"He's across campus just now. Is he expecting you?"

"No, I don't think so. I'm Traveler McGale, Daniel McGale's father."

"Oh," said the young receptionist, "Well, he should be back in...not too long. You can...Would you like some coffee?"

"That I would. Thank you."

"How do you take it?"

"Just black."

"Black it is," chirped the receptionist as she rose and opened a heavy oak door behind her.

Trav cupped the warm mug in both hands and looked out the big front window at the falling snow. *What the hell am I doing here? How do I begin the search? Maybe I should just turn around and go home.*

The front door opened, letting in a rush of February air and Dan O'Malley along with it. The headmaster veered straight to Trav.

"Mr. McGale. Good morning. Come on in," he said, guiding Trav by the elbow into his office.

Trav guessed that the receptionist had called the headmaster on his cell phone to alert him to his unscheduled visitor. O'Malley invited him to sit with him in the big armchairs by the fireplace.

Trav began, "I'm sorry I didn't call to let you know I was coming up."

"That's quite alright," O'Malley said warmly. "Is your wife with you?"

"No. It's just me."

The receptionist knocked twice, then let herself into the room.

"Mr. O'Malley, would you like something?"

"Yes, tea. Thank you, Claudia. More coffee?"

"Yes. Thanks," said Trav.

As the door closed, the headmaster turned back to his visitor.

"Call me Dan, please. May I call you..."

"Trav."

"Trav. Well, Trav, I know only too well what brings you, so I won't ask. We have no new information since our last talk on the phone."

"I'm sure you would have called," said Trav. "I just drove up to see if I could track him down, try to find out what's going on with him."

"I know it's terribly worrisome."

Trav drained his mug.

"That may be the understatement of the year."

Claudia came in with a saucered cup of hot tea and a plastic pitcher of coffee. She placed the tea next to the headmaster on the small table between them as Trav held his mug to Claudia for a refill.

"Thank you."

"You're welcome."

Claudia turned and once again closed the door behind her.

O'Malley squeezed a lemon wedge over his tea.

"When you and Martha brought Daniel up here, did you meet Frank Quillen?"

"Who?"

"Frank Quillen. He's one of our English teachers. Our best teacher, in my opinion. You met some of the faculty. I thought maybe you met him." O'Malley sipped his tea, then continued. "Frank knows this place very well. He was a student here. " O'Malley took another sip, pausing for effect. "He was a student here before he ran away with two other boys."

Trav looked intently at the headmaster.

"Yes," said O'Malley. "He was a handful alright."

"How long was he a runaway?" Trav asked.

"Well, it wasn't..."

"Seven weeks?"

Trav felt for a moment as though he were back in court cross-examining a witness.

"No. I don't think it was that long."

O'Malley stopped and took some time to bob his tea bag. "Let me tell you a little more about the way we see things up here. Burson-Mann has been at this business a long time. We're not perfect, that's for sure, but we've been around the track a few times. We treat our students like adults..."

"But they're kids," Trav interrupted. "They're not adults."

"No," said O'Malley. "they're not. But they will be very soon and they all want desperately to be grown up. And so we believe the best way to help move them to that point is to treat them the way you and I would treat one another."

"And what is your liability if something were to happen to a student out there?" Trav asked, pointing out the window, noticing the snowfall, now heavier and wetter.

O'Malley looked over with the expression of a teacher quizzing a student.

"Have you read the liability clause in your contract with us?"

Trav always counseled his clients to 'read the fine print.' But the cobbler has no shoes and Traveler McGale, the lawyer, had not read the liability clause in the contract. He could infer, however, from the headmaster's relaxed demeanor that the school bore no responsibility for anything that might befall Daniel off campus as a runaway.

"These kids are angry. They're scared. They're confused. But they have to sort things out for themselves and they have to experience the consequences of their actions."

"But Daniel is just…"

"Daniel is just seventeen. I know. Seventeen for another month. We get all kinds of kids up here and Daniel is the kind that…"

"The kind that what?"

The headmaster again took to his tea, clearly considering the best way to respond. The he said, "Daniel is one of those. I can't teach him. You can't teach him. The world has to teach him."

"What the hell does that mean?" Trav asked hotly.

"It means just that. Running after him, trying to save him won't be very productive, in my view. The only teacher he will heed is his own life experience. And even that is not assured."

Trav thought about that for a minute then shifted the conversation.

"I'm going to try and find him," he said.

"I know you are."

"What would you recommend?"

"Well," said O'Malley, shifting in his chair. "what I would continue to recommend is that you leave him alone. But if you are determined to search, I would go down to Brewenton. We're not even sure he's there, but that's where they usually go. Go to the shelters. Go to the Salvation Army. Ask around. Go to the library."

"The library?" Trav struggled to picture his son voluntarily darkening the door of a library.

"Sure, the library. It's open to the public. It's warm and quiet. It has bathrooms and it's a good place to sleep."

Still taken aback, Trav muttered under his breath again, "The library?"

The headmaster stood.

"I'm afraid I have a staff meeting in a moment. Good luck. You have my cell. If I'm tied up, call Claudia and she can get me right away."

"Right. Speaking of calling, do you recommend I call Daniel?"

O'Malley looked strangely puzzled.

"After seven weeks, I would have thought the phone company would have stopped service for non-payment."

"We've kept the bill current," said Trav. "We thought it important to keep it up in case, you know, just in case."

"Yes," said O'Malley. "I know. Well, sure. Call him if you choose."

Outside, the snow was coming down harder and Trav, driving south toward Brewenton, turned his windshield wipers to maximum. The black blades oscillated along with the bouncing to and fro of own indecision. *I'll call him. Let him know I'm here. Yes. No, that would push him further into hiding. Yes. No, I'll never find him just wandering around.* The wipers swing back and forth. Yes. No. Yes. No.

He pulled off the road and looked down at the small icons on his phone. There it is. Contacts. He scrolled down to Daniel. He looked up again at the snow beyond the oscillating wiper blades. *Yes. No. No, not now.* He turned off the Honda's emergency flashers and pulled back onto the southbound lane of the interstate. He selected at random the second of the five Brewenton exits. The cityscape before him was a dreary patchwork of browns, blacks, greys and tans splotched with a light patchy covering of fresh snow. *The powers that be up here must have outlawed all bright, cheery colors.* He stopped at a convenience store.

"Is there a shelter close by?" asked Trav.

The man behind the cash register was dark-complected with a thick, black shock of hair brushed to one side. Pakistani, mused Trav, maybe Indian.

"Shelter?"

"Yes, a shelter. For sleeping for homeless. You know."

"Ah, shelter." The man turned and pointed out the window down the road toward the center of the city.

"I think maybe five lights there is a big stone church, right hand side. Go left there, then on left hand side, two maybe three streets it is there. It is a sign say 'Angle House.'"

Trav thanked the man, bought two Snickers bars and left. He found the church eight traffic lights down the road and turned left. After five intersections, he saw it on the left: a one story building with large glass windows, obviously a converted retail store. *Angle House?* He drove past as slowly as the cars behind him would allow and looked at the small sign above the door: Angel House. He found a parking space around the corner and walked back to Angel House.

A muscular black man with a bald polished head sat at a small desk by the front door. He regarded Trav's fresh pressed khaki pants and L.L. Bean powder blue parka.

"May I help you?"

Trav stood in front of the desk, shoving his hands as far as they would go into the pockets of his parka. He peered past the man into a large room just visible down a hallway.

"May I help you?" the black man repeated. Trav's attention moved back to the man.

"I'm looking..."

"You're not looking for shelter for yourself, are you?"

"No," said Trav. "I'm looking for a young man named Daniel McGale."

The man with the polished head held his gaze and repeated what he had just heard.

"You're looking for a young man named Daniel McGale."

"Yeah," Trav replied. He searched the inside breast pocket of his parka and fished out a photograph of Daniel and handed it to the man. "This fellow. Have you seen him?"

The man held the picture between his thumb and forefinger and studied it for a moment. Then he looked up to Trav's face and studied it.

"You a cop?"

"No," said Trav. "I'm not a cop. I'm a father."

"Oh. Looking for your boy, huh?"

"Yeah."

The man handed the picture back.

"You see, mister, we're not allowed to give out any information on the guys here. 'Sides, we get a lotta folks coming through that door."

"So you haven't seen him," Trav said.

"I didn't say that. I said I'm not supposed to say. But if you look around this town, maybe you'll find him."

Their eyes met and held steady. Trav reached out his hand.

"Thank you."

"Good luck."

The snowfall had tapered to light, breezy flurries and the faint circle of a pale sun emerged behind thinning clouds. As he approached his car, Trav reached in his pocket and pressed the Unlock button on his car key. He hesitated. Then he slowly surveyed his surroundings: the street, the traffic, the people, and the buildings. He pressed the Lock button and turned around.

Trav walked for two hours, looking, fretting, thinking, hoping. He found the Salvation Army offices and went inside.

"May I help you?"

She was an open, pleasant sort, trim greying hair falling just to the collar of her heavy maroon sweater. He regarded her and her cramped, musty office space.

"I was looking for the Salvation Army shelter here,"

"We had to close our shelter down last year," she said. "Our funding just wasn't enough. The Lutheran Church's Angel House is close by. It's really the only men's lodging downtown here." She hesitated, then continued, "It's easy to find. I can give you directions."

"No. That's fine. Thank you," Trav said. "I'm not actually looking for shelter. I'm looking for someone who needs shelter."

The lady introduced herself as Cynthia Morrow. Trav told her about Daniel and about the school and the early morning when Dan O'Malley had called. He told her about his search and that he thought he didn't know how to search.

"Of course you know how to search," Cynthia said. "That's what you're doing right now. You cast your net, you talk to people, you follow leads. That's all you can do." She looked down and up again directly at Trav. "Was your son into drugs?"

"Yes. Was. Is, I think."

"You need to know there's quite a drug sub-culture here. Like most cities, I suppose. Kids mostly. Teens. But there are some older men involved. Dealers. They're not nice people."

"Where are they?" he asked.

"Here and there," Cynthia said. "But they tend to congregate down at Fordson and Dodge. There's a bar down there and some apartments over the bar. You wouldn't want to go down there ordinarily. But in your situation, you might want to."

"Thank you, ma'am," Trav said, extending his hand.

"You be careful."

# CHAPTER 12

# Wandering

He went first to the public library in the heart of the city. It was a relatively new building with elevators, large glass windows and soft lighting recessed from the high ceilings, and thousands of books. Of course, he was not looking for books. He took the elevator to the second floor and wandered through the stacks. In the fiction section, he turned down an aisle and then turned left. Against the wall on his right were a series of one-person study carrels. He looked down the aisle and froze. *Oh my God.* He held his breath. *It's him.* A young man with messed brown hair was sitting, his back toward Trav, four carrels ahead, his head buried in his arms on the desk. *Was he sleeping?* A dirty, olive-green Army surplus jacket hung over the back of his chair. Trav's heart pounded as he quietly walked forward. Coming closer, he saw an open book on the desk with the young man's left hand, palm down, on the page. It was a page of numbers and formulas. *Numbers? Math?*

He was now only a few feet behind Daniel. *Was it him?* He moved alongside and saw the sleeping face. It was not Daniel. He leaned against the end of the stack and stared at the young math student. A disembodied female voice spoke into the room.

"The library will close in five minutes. The library will close in five minutes."

The young man who was not Daniel roused himself, closed his schoolbook and reached down by his feet for his backpack. Rising, he glanced at Trav, not ten feet away, staring at him.

"What are you looking at?"

"Nothing," Trav said, "Sorry. I thought for a minute you were…"

The young man brushed by Trav and walked toward the elevator. Trav took the stairs.

On the way to his motel, he stopped to purchase a bottle of wine, a nice California cabernet. If he were here, Spear would like this wine. He wished, he *really* wished Spear were with him now. At least he had the wine.

He drew open the curtains on the motel room window. Winter stars glistened over a faint red Western horizon. There had always been, for him, a wash of melancholy at sunset time. He never knew why, but he hated being alone at the end of a day. As he watched the red glow fade into night, he pulled his cell phone from his pocket and pressed a name on his contact list. After five rings, the call tripped into voice mail: "You have reached the McGale's. We can't come to the phone right now. Please leave a message."

"Hi, honey. Just wanted to check in with you. I went to the school this morning and talked with O'Malley. They have no news, but he thinks Daniel may be in Brewenton. I'm there now. Looked around today. I'm tired, really tired." He paused, unsure of what, if anything, he should add. Then he said, "I'll call you tomorrow. I've got to charge my phone now. Love you. Good night."

He fished his cell phone charger out of his bag, plugged it into the wall socket and slotted the phone into the charger. He looked again out the window. Twilight was giving way to night and his loneliness had become a soft ache. He reached again into his travel bag, this time for his corkscrew. *Where is that goddamned kid? Why is he doing this to me?*

The digital clock next to the bed tripped over to 9:14. The cell phone, still in the black plastic cradle, was fully charged. The wine bottle was empty. Trav lay on the motel bed fully clothed. With alcohol in his veins and his cell phone off, sleep came easily. He had dreamed he was at a rustic summer camp on a hill overlooking the water, a lake, perhaps, or a coastal inlet. The camp's launch ferried people back and forth from the camp to the far side. The launch was now approaching the camp side and Trav wanted to cross over. He needed his life jacket and ran up the hill to retrieve it from his locker. Quickly now. The launch was coming. The locker combination? A ten, then a four. What was the third number? Hurry! It wasn't working. People were with him trying to help. The boat was going to leave without him. To hell with the life jacket! I can go without it. No, better play it safe. Come on, damn it! Ten, four, what? Ten, four...The launch was pulling into the dock down the hill.

Trav woke into a groggy consciousness. The clock read 1:52 am. He blinked. He rolled over, closed his eyes and drifted off into a restless, patchy sleep.

☙❧

In the morning, he undressed, showered, shaved and redressed in the same clothes. He waited until he had everything in order, then sat on the edge of the bed and turned his cell phone on.

"You have one new voice message."

"Got your message. I was at the club with Mary for some soup and salad. I'm glad you went to the school. That was good. You know how I feel about...I don't know sometimes what the right answer is."

Trav could sense a flatness in Martha's voice.

"I don't love what you're doing and I think you're rescuing and enabling, but I can't control you and you can't control Daniel. Call me tomorrow. Bye."

He left his bag in the room and walked to the motel office.

"I'd like to stay one more night."

It was a cloudless blue sky, a bitter cold morning. Trav climbed into his car and headed off in search of coffee.

He sat in a booth at the diner, a ballpoint pen in one hand, coffee cup in the other. With his index cards in the car, he was resigned to making notes on his paper napkin.

The waitress approached.

"Coffee?"

Trav looked up.

"Yes. Thanks."

She filled his cup and he looked back down at his 'plan' for the day.

*Go back to Salvation Army*

*Call Daniel?*

*Police?*

*Back to Angel House?*

*Text Daniel?*

*Go to the Bad Area?*

Not much of a plan. He sipped his coffee and regarded his notes. One definite action step, five possibles. *What the hell am I doing?* He finished his eggs and scrapple and drank more coffee. Maybe some other steps would come to him. None did. The waitress approached again.

"More coffee?"

"No thanks. I'm ready for the check."

"You got it." The waitress put the check on the table.

"Have a good one."

He drained his last swallow of now lukewarm coffee and stared straight ahead and into his own puzzled ruminations. He absently tapped the end of his pen on the table, trying to decide. *Might as well try.* On his cell phone, he slowly typed a text message.

*Daniel, thinking about you. Hope you are alright. PLEASE call.*

He looked at the message for a long time, then moved his thumb over the SEND button and pressed it.

"Done," he said aloud to himself. He left a five dollar bill on the table, paid the bill up front and headed back to the Salvation Army.


Cynthia looked up from her desk as the door opened.

"You're back."

"Good morning. Yes, I'm back." He suddenly felt shy and unsure of himself, not knowing what to say.

"How was your search yesterday?"

"Oh, nothing really. "I walked around town, went to the library."

"Did you call your son?"

"I texted him just this morning. No response yet."

"I see."

Trav came close to her desk and leaned forward.

"Can we talk for a few minutes? Do you have time?"

Cynthia turned back to whatever had been occupying her on her computer screen, pressed a key and looked up.

"Sure. I can take a few minutes. Have a seat."

Trav hung his parka on the back of the chair and sat. He retrieved his ballpoint pen and a few three-by-five cards from his shirt pocket.

"Can you tell me more about that bad area downtown?"

Cynthia put her elbows on her desk and intertwined her fingers under her chin.

"The bad area. "Yes. Well, let's see. I think I told you about the bar."

"What was the name?"

"Hooligans."

"Sounds appropriate."

"All too, I'm afraid," Cynthia said. "The building down there, it's a two-story, owned, I'm told, by a man named Larson, Josh Larson. He's in his late thirties, I think. Maybe forty. He's a shady character, let's just say that. He owns the building, the bar and has a few apartments over the bar he rents out or lets people use."

"And you think Daniel might be down there because?"

"Because you said he had been into drugs. Some say Larson is also a drug dealer."

He looked pensively at Cynthia who added, "I've also heard that he has some sort of arrangement with the police. Payoff for protection."

"I see."

"I can't vouch for any of this. Just what I've heard. I've never laid eyes on Josh Larson."

Trav was trying to think if there was anything else he should ask when his phone rang. It was Martha.

"Hey honey," he answered.

They talked for a few minutes. Trav told her about his meeting with O'Malley, about the library, Angel House, the Salvation Army and his conversations with Cynthia. He told her he had texted Daniel and that there had been no response. He told her everything, everything except his awareness of the bad area and Josh Larson.

"Bye. I'll call you," he said, then turned to Cynthia. "Sorry for the interruption."

"Quite alright."

"Well," said Trav, reaching behind him for his parka. "You've been great. I really appreciate your help."

"Come by anytime or call," said Cynthia, handing him her business card. "Good luck."

"Thank you."

Trav returned to his car, turned on the engine and waited. He waited for the engine to activate the heater. He waited also for a clue as to what he should do next. Too early to go down to the bad area. His exhaling breath clouded in front of him. He turned on the heater, feeling warm air. He rubbed his hands together, then shoved them into the side pockets of his parka. His left hand felt the smooth plastic surface of his cell phone. He took the phone out and looked at it for a long moment. He took a deep calm-yourself-man breath, then scrolled down his contact list to the Ds and placed a call which, after one ring, tripped into voice mail. His phone is off, he thought, or else the battery is dead.

"Daniel, its Dad. I'm up here in Maine. We need to talk. Call me. I'm on my cell."

He took in another long slow breath and exhaled through his mouth, puffing out his cheeks. He looked out the front windshield. Yesterday, he was angry that Daniel was not responding. Today, he was scared that maybe he couldn't respond even if he wanted to. *Goddammit!* He eased out of his parking space and the Honda led him throughout the morning on an aimless drive through town.

He parked at one point back at the library, went in and wandered again through the stacks. The math student wasn't there. *Unlike my son, he's probably in class where he should be.* There were a few older, indigent-looking men, clearly not much interested in reading, slumped in armchairs. As he pushed open the library's big front door to leave, his phone beeped an incoming text message. Trav's heart pounded and his stomach zinged. He stepped back through the door and out of the cold. Then he took a deep breath and read the message:

> *Hey Dad. Mom says you're up in Maine looking for Daniel. Good luck. Hope U R OK. BTW, I got an A on my history midterm. Love you, Eryn.*

He read the message again, then pressed REPLY.

> *Hey kiddo. Yes, trying to track him down. I'm worried about him. Great to hear about the A. Keep up the good work! Luvya, Dad.*

He pressed SEND, then double-checked his in box for any other new messages. There were none.

# CHAPTER 13

## *Hooligans*

It was almost noon when he opened the front door of Hooligans. He stepped in and onto a creaky, dirty, hardwood floor. A scattering of square wooden tables was arrayed in front of a long bar with a worn brass foot rail running its length. A man with a goatee and a short ponytail stood behind the bar drying a glass mug. He looked up at Trav.

"What's up, my friend?"

Trav slid onto a bar stool.

"Not much."

"Lunch?"

"I think so."

The bartender slid a menu in front Trav, who looked it over for a minute. Mr. Ponytail walked back to his only patron who, still looking at the menu, said, "I'll have bowl of the clam chowder"

"Anything to drink?"

"Heineken."

"You got it."

Ponytail walked to the far end of the bar, returned with a cold, green bottle of beer which he placed in front of Trav and then disappeared into the kitchen behind the bar. Trav took a long, slow swallow, savoring the feel of the cold brew flowing down his throat. He took another swallow, wondering how to make his approach.

Ponytail re-emerged with the clam chowder. "You all set?

"Uhm. Maybe another Heineken."

He was thinking fast how to keep Pony-tail with him, how to engage him in conversation.

"You serve dinner here?"

"Sure."

"And how late do you serve?"

Ponytail laughed.

"I'll put it this way. We serve later than you want to eat."

Trav laughed too.

"You worked here long?"

"Just a year or so."

Trav was pretty sure Ponytail was not the owner, but probed anyway.

"You own the place?"

"Wish I did. Mr. Larson's the owner."

As Trav started on his chowder, he sensed Ponytail studying him closely. It was then the bartender's turn to ask questions.

"You're not from here, are you?"

"Why do you think that?"

"Never seen you before. We don't get many strangers just wandering in at seven-thirty in the morning."

Ponytail wiped his hands on a small dish towel.

"And you're not a cop."

Trav took a swallow of his Heineken.

"How do you know I'm not a cop?"

"Cause I know the cops around here."

"Maybe I'm new on the force."

Ponytail smirked.

"Funny lookin' uniform. Let me get you your beer."

He walked to the far end of the bar, sauntered back with a second cold Heineken and regarded Trav closely.

"Maybe you're a detective. Maybe a private detective." He paused. "You lookin' for someone?"

Trav reached for his new beer and slid it close to him.

"Why would you say that?"

"Folks come in here once in a while looking for someone," said Ponytail.

"And if someone were looking for someone, why would they be coming in here?"

The bartender shrugged, perhaps tiring of the verbal cat-and-mouse jousting, and turned back toward the kitchen door behind him. Trav stopped him with another question.

"Let me ask you something," he said. He reached into the pocket of his jacket. "It turns out I am looking for someone." He put his photograph of Daniel on the bar and looked up.

"Do you know this young man?"

Ponytail picked up the photograph and looked at it.

"Kinda looks familiar, actually. Not real sure."

Trav leaned forward.

"Have you seen him in here?"

"Mmmmm." Ponytail handed the picture back.

"Not sure."

Trav sensed the man knew more than he was telling.

"Not sure?"

"Yeah," the man said. "You might want to see Mr. Larson. Maybe ask him."

"Where's Mr. Larson?"

"Probably upstairs. That's where he lives."

Trav swiveled on the bar stool, searching the room for a staircase. There it was, off on the left side of the front door. He had walked right by it on his way in. He turned back to Ponytail.

"He lives upstairs, huh?"

"First door, right at the top of the stairs."

"You think he's there now?"

"Probably. He's not an early riser. And when he does get up, he's sometimes not in the best of moods."

Trav slowly consumed his chowder and second beer, contemplating his next move. Maybe he should go to the police before doing anything else. Maybe he should have gone to the police first.

Ponytail had disappeared into the kitchen again . A winter light shafted through dirty window panes. His cell phone beeped an incoming text. Trav closed his eyes and took a deep breath. He was afraid to look and afraid not to look. It was from his secretary at the office.

*Mr. M: Sorry to bother you on your vacation. Fran is looking for the Callahan file. Looked everywhere here. Do you by chance have it?*

Trav had told his law partner confidentially he was going to Maine to find Daniel, but he had told Jennifer he was off to New England to ski with some buddies. He pressed REPLY.

*Yes. Callahan file is at home. Sorry about that. Pls call Martha and ask her to drop it by. TM*

He pressed SEND and drained the last swallow from the green bottle. Ponytail left the tab on the bar and reached for the chowder bowl and empty bottle.

"Thanks," said Trav. "I'm Trav, by the way."

Ponytail replied, "I'm Ferguson. Folks call me Fergy."

"Thanks, Fergy. I appreciate your help."

"Not a prob."

The bill was fourteen dollars. Trav left two tens and a five on the bar and headed for the stairs by the front door. The steps creaked and the wooden handrail wobbled in his hand. He stood on the narrow landing in front of a dark forest green door with no markings on it. He raised his hand to knock, then hesitated. Was he doing the right thing?

When he was a teenager, his father used to say to him, 'You can't always make the right decision, but doing nothing ain't never the right decision.' Trav would discover later there are times in a man's life when doing nothing is, in fact, the right decision. But on this day, standing in front of the dark green door, he was too preprogrammed not to do nothing. Trav knocked, but there was no response. He knocked again.

"Who is it?"

"Mr. Larson, my name is Trav McGale I just had lunch downstairs. Fergy said you lived here and I'd like to talk with you for a minute."

There was silence. Then the voice behind the door asked, "What about?"

Trav hesitated.

"I'm looking for someone. Fergy said you might be able to help me."

"Wait a minute."

Trav waited ten minutes. He heard water running, then what sounded like the sliding of a chair. Finally the door opened. Larson was a short, stocky man with a swarthy, Mediterranean complexion.

His black, crew-cut hair was not much longer than his several day-old growth on his face. He regarded Trav with an expressionless gaze.

"What can I do for you?"

"I'm looking for someone. Fergy downstairs said you might be able to help."

"He did, did he?"

Larson looked unblinking at Trav.

"What's your line of work?"

Trav didn't want to tell him he was a lawyer. Lawyers and cops made people like Larson nervous.

"I'm in the shipping business," he lied. "Live down near Baltimore."

Larson puckered his lips.

"Baltimore, huh? You're a long way from home, aren't you?"

Trav nodded.

Larson continued, "Folks come up here for fun in the summertime. Not in the winter."

"No," said Trav. "I'm not here for fun." He pulled out the photograph. "Have you seen this young man?"

Larson held the photo, looked at it casually and handed it back to Trav.

"Yeah. Danny boy. I've seen him."

Trav felt a chill along the back of his neck. His stomach churned.

"When? How recently?"

Larson shrugged lazily.

"Oh, maybe a week or two ago. He used to hang out downstairs some."

"A week or two ago. Not since?"

"No."

"Do you know where I might find him?"

"I do, actually." Larson said.

Trav hung in midair, waiting with fear and hope for Larson's news."

"He's in jail."

Trav, stunned, felt himself pushed back by an invisible wind.

"Jail? How do you know?"

Larson again shrugged.

"Not sure how I heard. Just the buzz around."

Trav would learn later that Larson, like Fergy at the bar, knew more than he was telling.

"Why is he in jail?"

"Some drug charge, I think. Not real sure."

Trav's mind raced. *This is just a bad dream. Can I wake up from this?*

"Do you know Daniel?"

"Not really." Larson said. "Just seen him downstairs once or twice."

Trav looked down at the photograph that was now back in his hand.

"Which jail?"

"Only one in town," said Larson. "Brewenton City Jail. Four-ten Harbor Street."

*Interesting*, thought Trav. *How many people know the street address of their local jail by heart?*

"Four-ten Harbor Street," he repeated. "Where is that?"

"I'll give you a hint," said Larson, his tone turning a bit nasty. "Harbor Street is by the harbor. Down the hill 'til you get to the water."

Trav looked down again at the picture of his son. *Jail? Jesus!* He looked up again at Larson.

"Thanks," he said weakly.

"No problem," Larson said curtly, closing the door.

Trav moved quickly down the stairs and pushed open Hooligans' front door. Out in the glare of the winter sun, he heaved in a full breath of the sharp air and walked quickly to his car. He put both forearms on the steering wheel and rested his chin in his wrists. He closed his eyes. *Calm down*, he tried to tell himself. *Just calm down. One step at a time.*

He reached for his phone and called Martha. She picked up on the third ring. He told her about Hooligans, Fergy and Larson, his conversation with Larson and that he was in the car getting ready to drive to Four-ten Harbor Street.

"How long has he been in jail?" Martha asked with rising anxiety. "And why didn't he call us? You're allowed to make a call from jail, aren't you?"

"I don't know," Trav said impatiently. "I don't know any more than I told you."

"I wonder if I should come up and..."

"Honey, just hold on."

Trav had initiated the call but was now anxious to end it. He wanted to get going down the hill.

"I'll call you as soon as I know what's going on."

"Okay. Call me right away, okay?" He could hear the fear and weariness in her voice.

"I will. I love you."

Martha's voice was now barely above a whisper. "Love you too."

# CHAPTER 14

## Four-Ten Harbor Street

Trav pushed open the double glass doors and walked straight ahead to the Information Desk. A young female in a dark blue uniform looked up.

"May I help you?"

"I understand you have a Daniel McGale, a seventeen-year-old, in custody?"

The woman turned to her computer, pressed a few buttons, and then studied the screen. Still looking at it, she said, "Yes."

"Can I see him?" Trav asked.

"And you are?"

"I'm his father."

The woman, with a bored I've-done-this-a-hundred-times demeanor, pushed a clipboarded form under the glass.

"You can fill this out. We'll tell him you'd like to see him. Visiting hours are four to five. Thirty minutes per visitor."

Trav completed the form, handed it to the woman and left to wander through town until four. His cell phone double-beeped, signaling an incoming text message. He reached for his phone, more at ease this time because he knew it would not be Daniel. He pressed a button and looked at the small glowing screen.

*Hey wuz up? Any word from Danny? Luv U lots. Thrill.*

Trav's twin sister lived in Ashville, North Carolina. Divorced, she got by in a modest up-and-down way, running her small art and pottery shop.

☙❧

Traveler and Trillium were born a few minutes apart. She came into the world pink and squealing with newborn health. Her brother followed her out blue-gray, limp and quiet. Through the trauma of birth, the life-giving umbilical cord had become wrapped around the boy's neck, producing a stillborn twin. The doctors worked frantically. He was, in fact, not quite stillborn. Through some bountiful mix of medical skill and mysterious grace, air was moved into tiny lungs, a tiny heart began to beat again and this newborn—dead, then brought to life—was rushed down a hall to an incubator.

A kindly, balding pediatrician had told Mr. and Mrs. McGale that the situation was grave, that he could not be optimistic that the boy would live through the night. But he did and he lived through seventy more nights in that incubator. He lived and he grew and he became strong. Eight years later, when both were thriving children, Trillium teased her twin that he was 'retarded 'cause he came out puny'. Traveler responded with a fist to the mouth, which broke two teeth. The events of their birth day were never mentioned again.

Their father delighted in telling anyone who would listen that his daughter and son were named, respectively, after a beautiful flower and an insurance company. Samuel McGale was a Civil War aficionado and an admirer of General Robert E. Lee and Lee's faithful steed, Traveler. And so occasionally, the father would vary his tale, saying his twins were named after a beautiful flower and a horse. Trill was often tempted to call her brother Horse, but demurred for fear of losing more teeth. Trav, of course, soon tired of his father's mean-spirited jokes, but learned to endure them with stoic silence.

As a toddler, he not only couldn't say Trillium, he couldn't get his sister's nickname quite right. So Trill came out Thrill. In spite of the occasional sibling rivalry and teasing, Traveler and Trillium were not only close, they became embedded parts of each other's souls. It

78

was not until they headed in different directions for college that a separation, a good and healthy separation, began to take form.

During Trav's time in Vietnam, Trill slogged through long months of worry. She wrote him—almost daily—long rambling, upbeat chatty missives, never mustering the courage to pen the words in her heart of love and longing and fear that she might lose him. Later, during Trill's long siege of marital struggle, the fighting, then the separation, the short reconciliation and finally, the divorce, it was Trav, always Trav, if only by phone or text, that was her home base of safety and her refuge.

ఆ౷౷

Standing in the parking lot of the jail, Trav again read his sister's message, then hit REPLY.

> *I'm in Maine. Daniel's in jail. Will see him, hopefully, later today. Relieved and scared at the same time. Will fill you in. I love you. T*

In less than a minute, she responded.

> *Keep me posted. Praying for you all. I am tired lately. So tired. Talk soon. Luvya.*

He read the message twice. Tired?

> *Yeah. Me too.*

He closed the phone, pulled his jacket collar up close against the wind and walked toward the river.

It was twenty past four. He shifted his weight uncomfortably on the old folding metal chair and looked again through the glass window, waiting, hoping for his son to appear. Most of the other visitors were already in conversation with their inmates.

Trav waited. He looked again. Maybe he didn't want to see his father. *Am I doing the right thing? No, you're okay. You're doing what any father would do.* But a part of him wasn't sure.

Suddenly, he became aware of someone behind the glass. His heart raced. His stomach churned. There he was. He watched Daniel move toward him. Faded, ripped blue jeans hung low on his hips, pant legs almost covering old black sneakers. His hoodie was a drab Army green. His hair, longer than Trav had expected, was mussed, but not outrageous. Daniel sat. He looked through the glass at his father. Trav tried to read his face. Daniel looked down at his fisted hands then back to his father.

"Hi."

"Hi, Daniel."

The search was over. All the anxious, sleepless nights. All the worried, inconclusive discussions with Martha about what or what not to do. Travs' impulsive decision to drop everything and drive to Maine and his dogged investigation through the streets of Brementon. And now? Now that he had finally tracked him down, Trav was at a total loss of words to say to his son. So, for a moment, he simply watched as Daniel unfisted his hands and purposefully laid them flat, palms down, in front of him. The knuckles on both hands were dirty and scabbed.

"How did you know I was here?" Daniel asked.

"I just poked around town. A couple of folks suggested I come down here." He decided not to mention Larson or the bar.

Daniel looked at his father with suspicion.

"Tell me what's going on with you, son,"

Daniel fisted his hands again.

"They set me up. It's not fair. They just..."

Trav interrupted. "Who set you up?"

Daniel took a long deep breath, then slowly began his story. He had gotten a job at the mall, he said. He had met some friends, staying here and there at night. Drinking? Yes, he was drinking some. He bought some marijuana from a guy downtown. He was short on cash then, but told the guy he would pay him back the following week. Then he lost his job and couldn't pay the debt.

"Next thing I know, the cops arrested me for selling drugs." Daniel looked directly at his father.

"I never sold drugs to anyone, Dad. Never! It's a lie. They just went after me cause…"

A voice on a loudspeaker broke in.

"Visiting hours are over. All inmates are to leave the visitation area immediately. Visitation is now over."

Daniel stood.

"It's not true, Dad. I swear!"

"We'll work something out, okay?" Trav said. "I'll be back tomorrow. Come right at four o'clock, alright? So we can talk."

"Okay. Tomorrow."

# CHAPTER 15

## Talking to Trill on Tax Day

Every year, Trav promised himself and Martha that he would get started on their taxes early and avoid the April crunch. Every year, it was a broken promise and this year was no exception. But backing out of the post office parking lot, Trav smiled, noting that at least he was posting their returns earlier in the day on the fifteenth.

As the greening up of another Pennsylvania spring began to take hold, he and Martha were enjoying another period of relative peace. Before leaving Maine, Trav had hired an attorney to represent Daniel and he and Martha had both flown up for the trial at the end of February. The prosecutor's case was devoid of any evidence of selling drugs or even attempting a sale. On advice of counsel, Daniel admitted to possession.

Daniel's lawyer had tried many cases before the judge and knew his pattern. If the defendant would agree to go directly into treatment or, in Daniel's case, back into treatment, he would be lenient. Trav recalled the judge's stern visage as he looked down over his reading glasses at Daniel standing before him.

"Young man," he said, "I understand from your attorney here that your parents have arranged for you to re-enter the school and the drug treatment program you ran away from."

"That's right."

Daniel's lawyer was sitting right behind him and whispered, "Yes, Your Honor."

"Yes, Your Honor," Daniel repeated.

The judged looked down at a ream of papers in front of him, pretending, Trav thought, to be reading. The courtroom was stone silent. The judge looked up again at Daniel.

"I am sentencing you to ninety days in jail, suspended, pending your immediate return to school and the resumption of your addiction treatment."

"Thank you, Sir,"

"Your Honor," whispered the voice behind him.

"Thank you, Your Honor," Daniel dutifully said.

The judge continued to stare impassively down at the callow defendant.

"Young man, your parents have set before you a way forward. You have a chance now to start things over. I hope you decide to take advantage of what you are being offered. If I see you again in my court, I promise you will not be heading anywhere else outside the Brewenton City Jail."

Trav hoped the gravity of the judge's message would register.

"Do you understand?"

"Yes, Your Honor," said Daniel, demonstrating that he was teachable.

The judge banged his gavel loud and hard.

After the trial, Trav and Martha drove Daniel straight to the school, placed him again in the capable hands of Headmaster O'Malley with a stern warning and headed south. On the way home, they talked about how all this, they hoped, had put a real scare into their son, how they thought he had learned his lesson, and that *this time* he seemed serious about turning his life around.

Trav, relieved to have gotten his annual missive off to the Internal Revenue Service with several hours to spare, pulled into the driveway, looking forward to a peaceful evening at home. It was not to be.

The house telephone was ringing just as he stepped through the front door. Martha picked it up in the kitchen. Trav, standing in the doorway next to the refrigerator, listened to Martha's end of the conversation.

"Hey! Great to hear your voice! Getting ready for the Easter Bunny?"

She paused, then said, "Yes, I think so. She's having a good semester. So how are things"

Another pause.

"Sure, just a minute."

Martha turned her head toward the doorway.

"Trav, its Trill. She wants to talk to you."

"I'll get it up front," Trav said. He entered their small den near the front door, picked up the phone and took a seat on the sofa.

"Hey, babe."

Almost an hour later, they were still talking. Trav, bringing their conversation to a close, said, "I love you. You're going to be alright... No, no, don't think that way. You're going to be alright. Now listen. I'm going to talk to Martha right now. Okay. Please get on the phone. Do it tonight. Book a flight and call me tomorrow...Promise? Okay, then. I love you...Call me in the morning, now...okay. Bye."

Trav let the phone slip into its cradle. He closed his eyes. A ball of fear swelled in his chest. He walked slowly back to the kitchen where Martha was stirring something on the stove.

"You guys sure were on the phone a long time. Good talk?"

Trav didn't respond. He walked to Martha, putting his hands on her shoulders and touched his forehead to hers. Martha looked up and into her husband's face. His eyes were tired. His lips had a quiver.

"What?"

Trav took a deep breath.

"She has cancer."

"Cancer?"

"I think it's serious. It's in her stomach...spread around...maybe the liver too."

Martha put her hand to her mouth.

"Oh, Lord! Oh!"

"She's terrified."

"Oh...of course."

"Honey, I told her..." Trav stopped then started again. "This all came just now like a ton of bricks. I told her—I guess I should have talked to you—but I told her to come up here. You know, she's all alone down there. She can get in to see a specialist and we can..."

Martha reached for his hand and held it tight.

"Of course. Of course. She mustn't be alone." She leaned forward to hug Trav. She buried her head into his chest and cried.

"Oh, poor Trill."

Trav's mind was spinning. *Missing son. Angry, hurt daughter. Trill with cancer. Thanks, God. You Fucker! What's next?*

The three of them were standing at the gate waiting for her plane to arrive. Eryn and Martha were in a conversation, focused on one another. Trav, holding a large bouquet of blue trilliums, kept his eyes on the airport doorway through which his sister would pass. He walked over to the gate counter.

"Excuse me. Has the flight from Charlotte landed?"

The young lady in a dark blue uniform looked down at her computer screen, then up to Trav.

"Yes, sir. Landed. Pulling up to the gate right now."

"Thanks."

Trav walked to his wife and daughter.

"Plane's here."

&#x0a;&#x0a;🙖🙖

He turned again to watch the door and to wait. He and Trill were last together the previous May. Eryn had finished her spring college semester and was off at the beach with a gaggle of girls. After considerable grumbling and cursing, Daniel had agreed to go with his parents to North Carolina to visit Aunt Trill, who had secured use of a three-bedroom cabin on Lake Lure. An old Lightning-class sloop came with the cabin.

Martha preferred to read and hike. Daniel preferred to sleep and when he wasn't sleeping, complain about life, his family and the general direction of the universe. But Trav and Trill, most mornings and some afternoons, were out on the lake sailing. Some days, when the wind was right, they could sail on a starboard reach all the way to the far end of the lake and back to the cabin on a port tack.

It had been years since the twins had spent any considerable time alone. They reminisced about their childhood. They laughed and cried, remembering their father and his remote, loveless demeanor.

On their final day, they headed out after lunch, determined to complete one last sail to the end of the lake. On the return, the wind slackened, clocked around to the south and then died altogether. The sky was a royal blue. The surface of the lake mirrored glass. For two hours, Traveler and Trillium sat on the old Lightning sailboat in the middle of Lake Lure, North Carolina. Years later, he would hold the memory of that time, almost ahead of all others, as a true gem.

They talked about Martha and Eryn and Daniel. They talked about Trill's ex and Trill's loneliness. They talked about being together and being apart. They talked too about God and sorrow and courage and love. He still could see her, back and elbows resting against the gunnels, head arched way back looking up at the pristine white mainsail pasted against the cloudless Carolina sky.

Trav's hair had turned a salt-and-pepper grey. Trill's, perhaps with the aid of something out of a bottle, had remained a glowing reddish-brown. She had tanned quickly at the lake and she was as pretty as Trav had ever seen her, especially when she would smile her broad, warm smile or laugh without control.

Trav remembered thinking, watching her step on and off the boat, that she was thin. Thinner, certainly, than he recalled. He didn't know then whether to compliment her or to express concern. That week at the lake, he did neither.

An airline agent walked to the gate door and opened it. Trav looked into the now visible gangway, tightening his grip on the bouquet, hoping he would see the smiling Trill of Lake Lure but fearing, knowing, that he would not. Martha moved close to Trav and put her arm around his waist. The first passengers plodded through the door. Then more and more. *Where was she?* Ten more. Then twenty more. *Had she missed the flight?*

Trav started toward the gate agent to ask. Then he saw her. She was wearing faded blue jeans and a brown sweater, carrying her coat in one hand, pulling her wheeled carry-on in the other. He saw her scan the faces of those waiting for friends and loved ones and spot her twin. Her closed mouth opened to a wide smile and her face lit up. She waved a high, happy wave and quickened her pace toward them. Martha reached her first and the two women embraced.

"It's so good to see you," Martha said, her voice muffled in her sister-in-law's hair.

"You too, Marth."

They released and Trill moved on to hug Eryn, then her brother. She looked up at him, dropped her handbag at her feet, then slowly closed her eyes and put her arms up and around his neck. Trav clumsily extricated the bouquet of flowers from between them and hugged her.

"Hey, Trav," she whispered.

"Hey, Trill."

For a long moment, they just held each other. Pressing his one free hand against her back, he sensed a thinness, a delicate fragility. He pulled away.

"Here you are," he said, presenting the trilliums to Trillium. "These are for you."

His awkwardness endeared her, as always, to him. She laughed.

"I thought maybe you brought them for one of the flight attendants."

Martha chirped from behind them, "Don't give him any ideas, sis."

Trill poked her nose into the bouquet to take in the delicate fragrance.

"Awwwww...how sweet." She then looked up again at Trav.

"Thank you."

"You're welcome." Trav looked down at her wheeled carry-on.

"Is this all you brought?"

"No. I've got a checked bag."

Trav reached for her carry-on and Martha reached for her sister-in-law's hand. The four of them turned and began their walk toward baggage claim and into Trill's fight to stay alive.

☙❧

They put her in Daniel's room. After unpacking, she came downstairs for a supper of Martha's homemade soup and a spinach salad. They sat together, blowing quietly on spoons full of hot soup and talking gaily about pretty much everything, everything except Trill's cancer. Later, after warm apple pie, Eryn went out with friends. The remaining three moved, with their coffees in hand, into the Room of the Flying Chair and talked. Now, they talked about cancer.

The doctors in Ashville had made a small incision, just exploratory. It was in her belly, large intestine mainly. The cancer had metastasized and spread. They were worried especially about the liver and kidneys and wanted to operate immediately. Trill had held them off, saying she was flying to Philadelphia to be with her brother and would focus on next steps up there.

Trav, relying heavily on Spear's guidance, had identified a highly regarded thoracic oncologist. The next morning, he drove Trill to see him.

# CHAPTER 16

## Cinco de Mayo

Warm afternoon light shafted through the young foliage of the oak and hickory trees. All of the soft red impatiens that bordered the flagstone patio were in full bloom. Spear was sitting outside reading. Hearing footsteps behind him, he page-marked and closed his book. It was Trav, of course, who pushed aside a low-hanging pine branch and stepped onto the patio.

"The good Doctor Robespiere, I presume."

Spear, not bothering to stand, extended his hand back over his head.

"The very one." He waved his hand toward a black wrought-iron chair.

"Sit. What's your poison?"

Trav puckered his lips and thought for a moment.

"How about a cold Dos Equis?"

"I don't have Dos Equis," Spear said flatly.

"What?" Trav said in mock surprise and disappointment. "Today is Cinqo de Mayo."

"That it is," said Spear. "I still don't have Dos Eqius."

"Well, then. A Corona."

"No Corona."

"A Margherita?"

"No Margheritas."

"You just really don't give a shit about Mexico's Independence Day, do you?"

Spear laughed.

"That's a pretty safe assumption."

He laughed again, stood and headed for the back screen door. Trav leaned back in the old patio chair and closed his eyes, letting the spring sun warm his face. Spear re-emerged with two cold beers brewed and bottled in the good old USA. Handing one to Trav, he said, "Haven't seen you in a while. How's life on the toney side of the loop?"

Trav took in a large swallow.

"Never dull, that's for sure."

They sat in silence for a minute. Then Spear, looking at the beer can on his knee, asked, "How's Trill? I think about her every day and I am praying for her."

"I appreciate that. We all do," said Trav. "She's managing as best she can, I guess. She hates the chemo."

"Who wouldn't."

"I mean she really detests it. It makes her nauseous. It kills her appetite. Fatigues her. But she's a real trooper. We've basically made Daniel's car available to her and she insists on driving herself to the hospital for her treatments. Martha and I want to drive her. But no. She doesn't want to be any more of a burden, she says. She can drive, she says. She's as stubborn as a mule."

Spear gazed up at the high limbs of his big hickory.

"Gosh, you're not stubborn at all. Hard to believe you two are twins."

Trav caught the playful sarcasm.

"Yeah, I know. But seriously, she's is in fragile shape. She is thin as a rail and she's weak. She doesn't have to be so damn stoic about all this."

"No, she doesn't have to be. But she is fighting for her life right now and that's part of the only way she knows how to fight."

"Well, the chemo ends in a month, thank God."

Spear looked over at his friend.

"Want another?"

Trav tapped the now empty can on the wrought iron.

"Sure. Why not?"

After his second laconic shuffle into the house, Spear sat, handed Trav his second brew and asked, "What do you hear from Daniel?"

"Thanks for asking. I guess he's doing okay. We have a scheduled call with him and his counselor every week. Tomorrow afternoon's the next one."

A cardinal swooped over the patio and perched himself on Spear's split rail fence. The bird perused the scene, flitted and twisted, then flew high up into the tall hickory.

"He's supposed to finish his rehab in July," said Trav.

"Do you think he's serious or is he just going through the motions?"

"Well, he's still there, isn't he?"

"Sure. But he knows if he leaves before finishing, he's looking at more jail time up in Maine."

"Well, technically, the judge's proviso was that Daniel return to the school, not that he finish."

Trav shrugged.

"All I know is he's there. Just have to see what happens. You know, with everything going on with Trill and Daniel up in Maine and the office and all. I just get up in the morning and do the best I can all day, then get up the next day and start all over again."

Spear looked over at his friend.

"That's all you can do. That and pray."

Trav shrugged. "Sure. That and pray. Why not?"

Spear looked up into the spring sky, closing his eyes and allowing the sunlight to wash over his face.

"Yes, why not, indeed?" he said softly.

Both men were quiet now. A crow cawed from a distant tree top. A fly buzzed around the patio table. Spear opened his eyes, leaned forward in his chair and reached for his beer. He took a swallow, leaned back again raised a new subject. Actually, it was a subject the two of them had discussed before, but not recently. He spoke with his eyes still closed facing up to the sun.

"Did you ever write to that hospital down in North Carolina about your birth?"

"I did," said Trav truthfully. "Just last week. Asked them to send me any records they had."

Trav had not raised the subject since Spear first suggested the idea, nor had he discussed it with Martha. But he had long harbored a gnawing sense that there was something missing in his birth story. It was just a feeling, but the feeling was strong enough that he was motivated to search out the name and address of the hospital in Charlotte, to call the hospital and to follow that up with a letter.

Interesting," Spear said. "I thought you had forgotten all about it."

"No, I remembered. My guess is that it will say pretty much what I already know."

"Might," Spear said. "But you never know."

Trav stood. He took another swallow of his second beer. "Martha's out and Trill may be be waking up from her nap. I'd better run on."

He patted Spear on the back.

"Thanks. Catch up with you soon."

As Trav headed for the path back to the loop, his friend called over his shoulder, "You still journaling, aren't you?"

"Every day," Trav lied as he pushed the low branch aside and stepped into the woods.

# CHAPTER 17

## At the Hospital

The nurse put her hand on the doorknob, then hesitated and turned toward them.

"Just for a few minutes now. She really needs her rest."

"Okay," said Trav, following Martha into the hospital room.

The white bed sheets covered Trill to her shoulders. One arm lay above the sheets with an intravenous needle. She was asleep. Martha pulled a chair close to the bed and took her hand. Trav stood behind Martha. Except for periodic beeping of a monitoring machine, there was no sound. Martha softly caressed the back of Trill's hand. Trill's eyes fluttered. She made a low guttural sound. The machine beeped again. She opened her eyes and surveyed her surroundings.

She looked at Martha, then up to Trav.

"Hey," she said, almost in a whisper.

Martha smiled warmly and squeezed Trill's hand.

"Hey to you, sweet lady."

Trill looked around the room and then out the window.

"What time is it?"

Trav said, "It's afternoon. About four."

"I'm so thirsty. Can I have some something to drink?" Trill asked.

Trav moved to the side table. While he was pouring water into a small paper cup, Trill spoke again.

"What did the doctor say?"

Martha leaned in toward her. "Honey, they said we could only stay for a few minutes. You need your rest and..."

"What did the doctor say?" Trill repeated, this time with surprising energy and irritation.

Trav handed her the water.

"Here. Hon, there's plenty of time for..."

Trill stopped him.

"We talked about this, damn it! You promised me honesty. No bullshit. Remember? Now you damned well tell me what they. what did they say?"

She looked at her brother straight on, unblinking. The blue of her eyes was hard and clear.

Trav shifted uncomfortably.

"Honey, you know that..."

"Tell me, Traveler. You promised me."

He looked at his twin, struggling mightily to suppress the sadness and fear welling in his chest. *Breathe, man. Just breathe. Talk calmly.* He cleared his throat and sat at the foot of the bed, his hand feeling her ankle beneath the sheet.

"The surgeon said what your doctor at home said. The cancer is in your stomach. He took out a tumor that was against your intestine. But it's spread and a lot of it they couldn't get. They want you to stay on chemo so that..."

"What about the liver and the other places?" Trill interjected.

Trav looked down at his hand holding her ankle.

"The cancer is in the liver." He paused. "And your ovaries and uterus."

Trill looked at him for a long time.

Trav continued, "You are going to go on some stronger chemo and maybe some targeted radiation." Then, trying to muster as much confidence as possible, he added, "These docs here are the best. We're going to beat this."

The room was totally silent. Trill took another swallow of water. She looked at Martha, then back to Trav. She turned her head and looked out the window.

"Look," she said quietly. "A blue jay." She closed her eyes. "Such a pretty bird."

# CHAPTER 18
## Deja Vu

July was almost over. A blistering heat wave had swept into the Mid-Atlantic region. Trill was soldering on courageously and Martha and Trav along with her.

The early dawn of another hot day. Trill was asleep in Daniel's room, Martha and Trav asleep in theirs. The first grey light of dawn seeped under their bedroom window shades. The telephone rang. Trav grunted and reached for it as it rang a third time.

"Hello?"

"Trav?"

"Yes."

"Dan O'Malley here. Sorry if I woke you."

*Oh, for Chrissakes. Not again.*

Martha sat up.

"Who is it?"

Trav put his hand over the receiver.

"It's the school."

"The school?"

"Burson-Mann. Daniel."

"Good lord!" exclaimed Martha as she headed downstairs once again to get on the phone.

O'Malley was saying, "...yes, I know. I feel as though we've seen this play before."

Trav asked, "Is anyone with him?"

"No. As far as we can tell, he left alone this time," O'Malley said. "Sometime after midnight."

"Well," said Martha, from the kitchen phone, "He's on his own this time. We've done everything we can."

Trav tightened his grip on the telephone.

"That knucklehead. What is he thinking?"

O'Malley said, "Daniel is eighteen. He's a legal adult now. Even if we located him, we couldn't force him to come back here."

Neither parent said anything. Trav had his all too familiar sinking feeling in his stomach. A sinking feeling of powerlessness.

O'Malley continued, "I'm so sorry to be calling you at this hour and again with this news. My advice is the same as before. We will, of course, contact you immediately if we hear anything."

Trav could only think to quote his favorite philosopher, Yogi Berra.

"Seems like déjà vu all over again, doesn't it?"

"I'm afraid so," said O'Malley. "Goodbye."

Trav put his bathrobe on and went downstairs to the kitchen.

"What do we do now?"

"We can't let Daniel's shenanigans control us forever, "Martha said, her back to Trav. "We pray for him and go on about our lives."

She turned around and looked up at her husband.

"Coffee?"

# CHAPTER 19
## The Day Trill Went Away

Martha had everything ready. The breakfast table in the kitchen nook by the garden window was set for three. Large spoons lay on paper napkins. Orange juice and coffee mugs sat in front of small white plates. Trav came into the kitchen and put his brief case on the counter.

"Good morning."

"Morning, honey," Martha said. "Is Trill up?"

Trav seated himself and downed his orange juice.

"I hope so. She's got an alarm, you know, and she bristles when we get on her."

Martha absently stirred the pot of oatmeal on the stove.

"I know. But she's in such a weakened state now. Poor thing. She's thin, she's nauseous. I just wish she would let us do more."

Trav looked out the kitchen window with tired eyes.

"You know when we were up on the hill last week waiting for the sunset, she fell asleep? How do you fall asleep sitting up on the side of a hill?"

"I think you should go get her up."

"I'm not going to get her up," said Trav. "But I'll tell you what I am going to do. I'm going to drive her to her chemo this morning."

Martha tapped drips of oatmeal off her wooden spoon and turned away from the stove to face her husband.

"She'll throw a fit. You know she will. You lent her Daniel's car and promised her she could use it and get herself back and forth to her appointments. You did, Trav."

"I know, but…"

"And besides, you said you had a client meeting this morning."

"Screw the damned meeting," Trav said. "I'm going to take her this morning."

Martha turned back to the oatmeal.

"You work that out with your sister. I'm just not sure."

"You're just not sure of what?" It was Trill asking as she walked into the kitchen.

Martha and Trav said in unison, "Good morning." Then Trav added, "How are you feeling?"

Trill moved deliberately but slowly over to the round table and sat. "I'm as well as I can be I guess with a stomach full of cancer and chemicals." She took a small sip of orange juice and slowly put the glass back down. "You're not sure of what, Martha?"

"Oh, we were just talking about stuff. I don't even remember now. How about some oatmeal? I've got raisins and brown sugar." Martha moved toward the table and ladled hot cereal into the bowl in front of Trill.

"Just a little. Please."

"You've got to eat, honey."

"Doesn't do any good if I eat and it all comes back up. Just a little."

Trill took a small spoonful. Rolling it slowly around in her mouth, she looked out the window.

"Beautiful day. Is it going to be hot?"

"Supposed to be in the nineties," said Trav.

Trill leaned forward to attempt another portion of oatmeal. Trav took a deep breath and tapped his index fingers on the table. Martha watched him and braced her back against the stove, knowing what was coming.

Trav looked over at his sister as she struggled to navigate more oatmeal down her throat.

"My morning is wide open today. How 'bout if I drive you to your treatment?"

"Why?" Trill asked, still focusing on her oatmeal.

"Because I have no appointments this morning and because…"

"Because you think I'm too weak," Trill snapped, finishing his sentence. "When I came up here you, and believe me, I can't tell you both how grateful I am that I'm here, that I'm not alone messing with all this by myself. But when I came up here, Bro, I said—remember?—that I hoped you would go on with your normal days. I don't want you to scurry around after me. I've been driving fine for two months, haven't I?"

"You have, Honey" said Martha, forgetting her promise to herself to stay out of this brother-sister dialogue. "You have. We just care about you and want to be okay."

"I know what you want," said Trill. "But here's what I want. I want to feel like a grown woman, a responsible adult, not an invalid. Just for a little while longer. I'm going to die pretty soon. Let's not pretend."

Trav jumped in. "Don't say that, Trill. Don't say that. Don't even think it! You're not going to die. You're feeling rotten now because of the chemo. The doctor said you would. But you are going to lick this. You've got to believe that."

Trill swiveled and glared at her brother. "What I believe is that whether I beat it or not, I'm not going to become a goddamned basket case that you two have to haul around."

"Trill, I'm going to drive you."

"No you're not!" She stood, knocking her chair over. Trav reached for it and she batted his arm away. She righted the chair, grabbed her purse from the kitchen counter and headed out of the house. Trav stood and started after her.

Martha grabbed his arm.

"Trav!"

He tried to wrestle free, but Martha held tight.

"Trav. Let her go. She's fighting with what she's got for some sense…" Martha hesitated, searching for that elusive word. "For some sense of…oh, God, I just feel so bad for her."

Trav put his arms around her and held her.

"I'm just worried."

"I know. I know. Me too."

They held each other for a long time

"I'm going to the office."

"Okay," said Martha. "I'm home all day. I'll be here when she gets back."

Forty-five minutes later, Trav was behind closed doors with a client. There was a soft knock on his office door. He ignored it. The knock again, firmer, a bit louder this time. The door opened. His secretary leaned in.

"I'm sorry to interrupt, Mr. McGale. Your wife is on the phone."

Trav looked up.

"Can you tell her I'll call her back in about thirty minutes?"

"She says it's urgent. She has to talk with you now."

*What's going on? Something with Daniel? What?*

"Okay."

The client graciously volunteered.

"I'll step out. I have to use the rest room anyway ."

Trav reached for the telephone.

"Martha?"

"Honey…" That's all she said. Trav listened, but there was no more. Then he heard a muffled breath, then a sob.

"Martha, talk to me."

There was that aching silence again.

"Trav you need to come home."

"What's happened?"

"Just come home. Please."

*Maybe something has happened to Daniel. Did she get a call from the rehab facility. Something with Eryn?* Then the fear he had kept at bay jumped into his throat. *Trill.*

"It's Trill. Isn't it?"

Martha's voice was weak and trembling.

"Yes."

He gripped the telephone tightly.

"I'm on my way. I'll meet you at the hospital. I'll be there…"

"No!" Martha shouted, "She's not at the hospital! Come home, dammit! Come home!"

The phone went dead, but Trav continued to hold it close to his ear. Then he put the receiver on his desk, put his hands in his face and closed his eyes. He breathed heavily through his hands and he prayed.

Fear always drove Traveler to prayer. It was like that on the muddy field that night. Trav had carried him back behind the tree line and the corpsman had immediately applied two tourniquets and a field patch onto the chest wound. Trav held his hand and talked and talked.

"You're going to be okay, man. You're going to be okay. Sorenson's here and he's got you covered. Medevac's on its way. Ten minutes they said. Just hang in there. Semper Fi, man. You're gonna be okay. Semper Fi!"

Vince had screamed in agony. Trav squeezed his hand. An explosion deafened all other sound and shook the ground.

"You're going to be okay. Oh, Jesus. Sorenson, what should we…"

The field medic had moved from the chest and was now working on the thigh.

"Please shut up, Sir. I don't have time now."

Vince screamed again. Then Trav heard it. Faintly at first, then the approaching sound. Thucka-thucka-thucka. He saw the lights of the helo descending, then he felt the wooshing air from the rotor blades. He leaned into Vince's face and shouted over the roar.

"Medevac's here, buddy. They're here. You're gonna be okay."

Two soldiers jumped from the helo and ran, heads bent down, with a stretcher. Trav jogged alongside the stretcher, his hand on Vince's shoulder. As they approached the helo, a soldier pushed Trav out of the way.

"We got him now. I need you to give us some space."

"I'm going with him." Trav shouted into the ear of the medic.

"No, sir. There's no room!"

The soldier pushed him away from the stretcher. Trav stood motionless in the eerie glow of the chopper's search light. His hand reached out to the roaring machine as it lifted off, banked and flew away. Trav dropped to his knees, touching two balled, muddy fists to his sternum.

"Oh, please God. Don't take him. Don't take him. Don't take him."

His friend died that night, but not from his wounds on the battlefield. Trav learned a week later that the helicopter had crashed, killing everyone on board.

❧❧

Alone now in his office, he prayed. He prayed hard and tight out of fear and desperation. He prayed again to the god he wasn't sure was there, the god with whom he was so angry, the god he couldn't quite quit. And as he did that night on the other side of the world, the words of his prayer were for one who was dying, but the plea from his heart was for his own soul.

Trav headed home, driving too fast. Fortunately, the car knew the way, because the driver's mind was busy juggling anxious thoughts. Come home, she had said. *Come home? Trill must be home. But why? What the hell?*

As he turned onto their street, he saw two black police cars parked in front of the house. What? Trav turned into the driveway. As he slammed the car into park, he realized his car was exactly where Trill parked Daniel's car when she comes home. It's Trill...come home... Daniel's car is somewhere else. His heart was in his throat.

He raced across the lawn and in through the open front door, lunging toward the missing piece of the puzzle that was already coming into focus. Martha, hands clasping a wet Kleenex, was sitting on the edge of the living room couch next to a uniformed police officer. Now Trav knew.

Martha stood and threw her arms around him.

"Oh, Trav. I am so sorry. I am so sorry. I shouldn't have said anything this morning. I am so sorry. Oh, God."

He held her close, stroking her hair. Softly he asked for an explanation of what he already knew.

"What happened?"

Martha released him and looked toward the police officer.

"Could you tell him?"

The officer glanced down at his notebook, then up at Trav.

"Sir. Earlier this morning, your sister was driving the blue Pontiac, the one registered in your name. Your wife said she was driving to the hospital for treatment. At the intersection of Grove and Lexington, in the intersection actually, another vehicle hit her."

Trav moved to sit in the big armchair facing the sofa.

"And do you know why the cars collided?"

"We're still investigating. Our guys are pulling together all the information we can, but..." The officer stopped.

"But what?" Trav pressed .

"Two eyewitnesses, pedestrians, said that your sister ran a red light. I'm not for sure just now. I'm just saying that's what they said."

Martha put her Kleenex to her eyes. Trav laid his hands on the armrests and stared a hypnotic stare into a void a few feet in front of him. Still looking down, he asked, "What about people in the other car?"

"It was an electrician's van. Just the driver. He's pretty badly injured. He's at the hospital your sister was trying to get to." The officer added, "The van T-boned the Pontiac."

"What does T-boned mean?" Martha asked.

Trav answered before the officer could speak.

"Hit broadside. It means she didn't have a chance." Then he turned to the officer and asked, "Where is my sister?"

"They've taken her, or they are in the process of taking her, to the morgue. I think they will need you to identify..."

Trav stood and walked toward Martha.

"I know. I know. Martha, let's go." He turned to the policeman. "Thank you, Officer, for your help on this. Here is my card with my home, office and cell phone numbers."

# CHAPTER 20

## Burial in Ashville

It was a beautiful little church, nestled in the woods just outside of Ashville. Speckled sunlight shafting through high foliage played through a soft summer breeze onto the gray granite stone of the chapel, stone hewn from the mountains of Appalachia a century ago.

After her divorce, Trill had talked often of her loneliness. So Trav was surprised at the large crowd present that morning for the funeral service. He shared his surprise with Martha.

"I'm sure she felt lonely down here after the split. But she had lots of friends. And everybody loved her. You know that."

"Yeah. Everybody except that jerk of a husband."

"Come on, now," said Martha, "Let's not go there today."

The pathway leading to the church was bordered on both sides with azaleas and mountain laurel. Eryn, looking like the beautiful young woman she was growing into, was dressed in a smart black suit and followed a few steps behind her parents. She reached into her purse and fished out her dark glasses. A clergyman was standing, Bible in hand, at the entrance. He was young, maybe forty, Trav guessed, tall, thin with curly brown hair. He nodded at Trill's family walking up the path and headed out to greet them.

"Hello," he said extending his hand. "You must be Travis and Martha."

Trav, as he had a thousand times before, resisted the urge to say, "I'm Traveler, not Travis," and instead simply replied, "Good morning."

"I'm Don Wheeler. After talking with you both on the phone, it's nice to connect faces with voices."

Martha introduced Eryn to the pastor.

"Nice to meet you Eryn."

"Yes. You too."

Reverend Wheeler turned back to Trav and Martha.

"Is your son with you?"

Trav felt his jaw tightening.

*This day is bad enough. Why the hell did he have to ask that question?*

"No, he's not."

The minister paused for a moment, as if expecting more, but none of the family members said anything further.

"Well," said the minister, handing a one-page, front-and-back program to each of them, "here is the order of service. I trust it is exactly what we discussed on the phone."

Martha and Eryn looked over the program. Trav rolled his into a small cylinder and clasped it, unread, like a baton in his hand. He looked up through the towering trees, wishing he could stay in the sunlight, knowing, though, that he must move inside the heavy stone walls. He moved closer to Martha and gently placed his free hand at the small of her back.

"Shall we?"

Eryn moved up next to her father and reached for his wrist just above the baton.

They sat in the front pew. Martha leaned over to Trav and whispered, "Isn't this a beautiful church?"

Trav nodded. Flowers, arranged on either side of a small, roughhewn wooden cross, adorned the table. *It is beautiful*, he thought, *but it's small. Everything is so close.* Something in him wanted to back away, to be there but further back. He had been placed right up front, right into the maw of his own powerlessness. He took a deep breath, unrolled his program and started to read.

The organist finished the preliminary music and paused, letting the momentary interlude signal the beginning of the service. He began again, playing an upbeat piece of music. A pretty young woman, with long straight strawberry blond hair that cascaded over her navy blue choir robe, stood. She sang with a pure, easy soprano voice:

*"I danced in the morning when the world was young*
*I danced in the moon and the stars and the sun"*

Martha leaned over and whispered to Trav, "Trill just loved this song."

*"Dance, dance, wherever you may be*
*For I am the lord of the dance said he."*

The hymn ended. Moving in smooth tandem, Pastor Wheeler stood and stepped forward as the strawberry blond stepped back and sat down. The pastor stepped to the center of the church and stood directly in front of the big oaken cross.

"Welcome all to Saint Luke's On The Mountain. We are gathered this morning to celebrate the life of Trillium Coe McGale. Jesus said 'Whom so ever believeth in Me shall not die, but shall have everlasting life.'"

A woman, one of Trill's close friends in Ashville, rose from her pew, walked to the pulpit and read from Paul's Letter to the Corinthians. Martha then followed and read from the Gospel of John. The reverend rose and spoke, not from the pulpit, but in a warm, informal manner, standing down at the level of the congregation. It was evident he did not know the deceased very well and had gleaned most of his material through his long distance conversations with Trav and Martha. But it was a good homily.

The time was drawing near. Trav wiped perspiration from his brow. As the minister began to wrap up, he reached in his breast pocket and touched the folded paper. Martha leaned into him and whispered in his ear. "Are you sure you want to do this? If you feel that...I can read it for you, you know."

"Its okay," he whispered back, looking straight ahead.

Reverend Wheeler took his seat as Trav stood and walked slowly to the pulpit. He unfolded his paper and placed it flat in front of him and looked out at those gathered. *Just breathe. Just breathe and read the words you wrote on the paper.*

"Good morning. I am Traveler, Trill's brother. On behalf of my wife,

Martha, and our daughter, Eryn, I want to thank all of you for being here this morning. It means so much to us to see so many who knew and loved Trill."

He continued in a strong, controlled voice to read his remarks, describing some of Trill's best attributes, talking about her love of art and keen sensitivity to beauty. He talked about her move down to North Carolina and how she had come to love Ashville and how it had become her home. He then stopped for a moment and looked down at his paper. It was a long, awkward pause. Martha thought perhaps he had lost his place in the text. In fact, he had his place exactly in the text, the last paragraphs which he could read but could not speak. He looked up again and out at his audience and ad-libbed.

"Trill was a wonderful friend and sister. Thank you all so much for being here with us."

Trav folded his paper awkwardly and stuffed it in his pocket. He brushed one hand under his eye as his stepped down from pulpit.

Had he been able to maintain control and read on, he would have said, "Trill and I were not just brother and sister. We were twins. We were so much a part of each other. I have long struggled with religion. I think there is a god. At least I hope there is, but It is all very mysterious to me. But I can tell you one thing: If there are angels in this world, my sister is surely one of them. I love you, Trill."

He returned to the pew and sat as Martha reached for him. He gripped her hand tightly and bit his lip. As the organist started, the congregation rose.

*"Amazing grace, how sweet the sound,*
*That saved a wretch like me*
*I once was lost and now have found"*
Martha held his hand now in both of hers.
*"Twas Grace that taught my heart to fear.*
*And Grace, my fears relieved."*

The dam broke finally and Trav wept uncontrollably.

# CHAPTER 21

## *On the Beach*

*What kind of a god are you? All-powerful and you love us? Why then all the heartache?*

Trav stared down at what he had just written, then added, *Maybe your first time running the universe?* He slapped the notebook closed, tapped the point of his pen on its green cover and tossed the notebook on the little pine table next to him. He took another swallow of cabernet and gazed out beyond the porch railing at the sea.

He had grown to dislike the daily journaling, but Dr. Ramos had strongly recommended it and, more importantly, so had Spear. Trav had promised he would write every day, at least two hundred words a day. At their last meeting, Dr. Curt Ramos had looked at his patient.

"You promise?"

"Yes, doc. I promise."

The young Veterans Affairs psychiatrist sighed.

"Trav, tell me. Why am I Curt when we're just talking and Doctor when the subject is journaling?"

Trav leaned back slowly in the faded white rocking chair, remembering that last session with his shrink. He remembered also that he had not answered Curt's question. Even though he stopped going to the VA after only three sessions, there was something, something in Trav that wanted to keep that promise.

He drained the last of the wine, stood and loped down the three porch steps, walking to the edge of the sea. The Carolina sun, low in the sky behind him, cast his long shadow to the water's edge. For idle amusement, Trav stepped forward, putting the shadow's head at the surf line, then began stepping forward and back, trying to keep the crown of the head moving back and forth in alignment with the ebb and flow of each wave. It didn't work. Shadow head was invariably either lagging or leading the foamy front line of the in-flowing surf.

With a tinge of frustration, Trav quit the game, turned south and started along the water's edge. Over the years, he had walked many beaches all over the world, meandering at times so far that he lost his way. Out of habit, he turned his head to fix on something that would mark his starting point.

His rented cottage stood alone on the desolate coast and he would have to walk more than a mile in either direction to come upon another man-made structure. He studied the profile of his cottage with care and without hurry, making a mental note of the double brick chimney rising against the north end of the house, with both caps silhouetted against a now brilliant, yellow-orange Western sky.

Ann at the real estate office had told him all about the cottage. It was built right after the Second World War, erected by the current owner's great uncle. The old man, Clemson Padgette, had served on a destroyer in the Pacific, returned to the island of his birth after the war, built a house on the beach and thereafter rarely ventured onto the mainland. It was said the man occupied himself fishing, doing odd jobs in the village and drinking bourbon. He reportedly pursued all three enterprises with equal measure of routine and perseverance. He never married.

The cottage, clad in faded grey cedar shingles, was a sturdy warren. Inside, the two bedrooms and the long, open general room boasted oiled, knotty pine paneled walls. Only the tiny kitchen had plaster board walls. To the right of the sink stood an old propane stove which, along with the two fireplaces, was the cottage's only source of heat.

Though he had only occupied the cottage for a short time, he had already developed a tender sensibility toward the place. In a way, it was becoming his friend, his companion. It was, of course, a mute wooden thing. But he had subconsciously given it a human personality, a female human personality. So, he made a mental note of the stubby chimneys protruding above the roof line, waved self-consciously to his friend and turned back to his evening walk along the sea.

The sun was below the dunes now and the deep blue of the Atlantic had faded to an evening grey-black. Waves rose, curled and broke in a briny crash, then raced in a flattened form onto the beach and toward Trav. The dark seawater swirled around his ankles and calves. The repetitive ebb and flow of the surf cooled his legs and soothed the restlessness within him. As he strolled south, he thought about his lot in life and about his time to date here on the North Carolina Outer Banks.

He absently scratched his cheek, feeling a week-old growth of beard. It had come in mostly grey, with uneven patterns of brown and reddish- blond. He hadn't planned to grow a beard. Rather, during his first day or two at the cottage while he focused on settling in, journaling, walking and finding bottles of good red and white wines, the beard was simply left alone to emerge unattended.

Trav at times had difficulty reading other people, their emotions, their true intent and their feelings toward him. But he was very good at other things. Other things like numbers. With no conscious effort, he could recall telephone numbers, his bank account number, the license plate numbers on his car and Martha's. And so it was effortless for him to recall that it had been twenty-six days since Trill had gone and now seventeen—sixteen and a half, actually—that he had been on Okracoke Island. It was three weeks, three weeks to the day, since they had buried Trill.

After their drive from Ashville back to Pennsylvania, Trav tried to settle back into his legal work and his regular routine. He tried, but rambling somewhat aimlessly through his day at the office, he couldn't get the idea out of his mind. Not the idea of Daniel, nor of Trill, nor the funeral, although these thoughts were all ever-present. No, on this day, it was a desire to leave, a gathering tug to get away that preoccupied him. At lunchtime one day, he walked out of the office alone to procure a sandwich. Returning, he asked his secretary not to disturb him. He entered his office and closed the door.

*Yes, indeed. I'm going to do this.*

He opened his computer straight away and searched for real estate agents on Okracoke Island. Still staring at the listing that appeared on the computer screen, he reached for the phone and called the number of the company at the top of the list. A woman answered after the second ring.

"Good morning. A Place at the Beach. This is Rachel. How may I help you?"

"Hi," said Trav, "I'm looking for a place down there to rent for a while."

"Just a moment, sir. Let me have you talk to one of our agents. Please hold a sec."

It was a few 'secs', then another woman came on the line.

"Good morning. This is Ann Sample."

"Good morning. My name is Trav McGale. I'm interested in renting a place down there."

"Well, sure, Mr. McGale. I would be happy to help you. Let me ask you: Have you been to our island before?"

"I was there a few times when I was a kid, but that was a few decades ago. I'm sure it's changed a bunch over the years."

"Actually," Ms. Sample said, "it probably hasn't changed as much as you think. Nine-tenths of the island is a national seashore and the big changes we get here are from storms."

"I'm sure. I remember the little town at the south end."

"It's still a little town. A bunch of pretty big new beach houses. But it's still little ol' Okracoke. Tell me what you're looking for."

"Well," said Trav, "I'd kind of like to be off by myself. On the beach if you've got anything."

"How many bedrooms?"

"One."

"One? Not many places down here with one. How about two or three?"

"Well..."

"When were you thinking of coming?"

"I was thinking tomorrow."

"Tomorrow?"

They talked back and forth about price, location and views. Trav wasn't explicit about his situation, but Ann Sample had experience reading between the lines and sensed she was talking to a man who for whatever reason wanted—needed—to get away from it all. She couldn't know what it all was and it was none of her business in any event.

They continued to talk and at one point, the real estate lady asked, "Is air conditioning essential for you?"

"Air conditioning? What?"

"Air conditioning. I mean central air. Modern."

"Well, why do you ask?"

"I don't know if this would interest you, but there is a very nice, older two-bedroom cottage a few miles up the beach. It sits off by itself. It's actually inside the National Seashore, but since it was built so long ago, they grandfathered it in. There might be a window air conditioning unit in one of the bedrooms. I could check to be sure."

Trav was putting together his own mental image of the place as she was describing it. He interrupted her.

"I'll take it."

◈◈

Later that day, Martha was thumbing through the day's mail at her little kitchen table when Trav walked into the house. She glanced at the clock on the stove: 4:52. The workday was over, at least for Trav. He appeared in the doorway.

"Hello," he said flatly.

Martha looked up over her reading glasses.

"There's my guy. How was your day?"

"Oh, samo, samo," Trav said, opening the refrigerator door and reaching for a bottle of white wine.

He asked Martha,"Want a drink?"

"It's a little early, don't you think? It's not even five," Martha said, slitting an envelope. "Maybe later."

"It'll be later soon. Come on."

"Oh, okay," she sighed.

Martha was keenly aware of her husband's sadness and made

115

conscious efforts to go the extra mile now to try and comfort him. They repaired, drinks in hand, to the family room and sat together on the couch. Trav took in the view through the new bay window, remembering the pieces of glass and splintered mullions.

"No word, I suppose, from the school or the police?"

Martha took a sip of her wine.

"No word."

She watched her husband, who was watching a blue jay perched on the bird fountain in their garden.

"I know you're still hurting," she said quietly. "Who wouldn't be? Is there anything I can do for you?"

Trav turned away from the window and faced Martha. *I am lucky to have this woman.*

"Yes," he said. "There is. You can try and understand and support me in what I want to say just now."

Martha looked at him quizzically.

"And that would be what?"

Trav turned back toward the bay window and looked for the bird that had disappeared. He felt Martha waiting.

"I want to go away for a few days."

He paused to savor a swallow of his wine. Martha didn't say anything.

"I'm just in a funk. I'm down about Trill. I'm down about Daniel. I get nothing from the job anymore."

He sighed, closed his eyes and leaned his head on the back of the couch.

"Just down about life right now."

"So you want to go away?"

Trav's eyes were still closed.

"Yeah."

"By yourself?"

"Yeah."

Even as he shared his plan with Martha, he felt conflicted. *Would it be a healthy change of venue to reflect, heal and recharge or a coward running away from his problems?*

"Where are you planning to go?"

"The beach."

"The beach? What beach?"

Trav told her about the call he had made from the office that afternoon. He told her about the cottage he had rented, that he had secured the firm's blessing to go and that hoped he might have hers as well. Martha looked down, picking at a loose thread on her blouse.

"How long do you plan to be gone?"

"I don't know, really. A few days. Maybe a week or two. I haven't thought this through all the way. I just feel in my gut that I need to go off and think and clear my head. Try to get back on track."

"Okay," Martha said quietly.

Trav reached over and took her hand in his.

"You sure you're okay with this?"

She hugged him and held him tight.

"I'm okay, I guess," she said, burying her face against his neck. "Just don't stay away too long."

Trav put his arms around her and held her close.

"I love you, Marth," he said, nuzzling his face in her hair. "I love you so much."

&#x264A;&#x2629;

The following afternoon, only minutes before *A Place at the Beach* closed for the day, Trav pulled up to get the key to the cottage and directions from Ann Sample. She walked with him out to his car and pointed down the street to a stop sign.

"Turn left at that intersection and go four point seven miles. The house stands off by itself. There's a little sign over the mailbox out on the road that says 'Padgette.' Call us if you need anything. Enjoy your stay."

And so began Traveler McGale's' time at the cedar-shingled cottage by the sea.

Now, he continued his walk by the sea. A blue-black curtain had crept over the water as a pale sliver of white moon emerged above the horizon. Trav angled slightly to his right away from the surf and onto the hard, still wet sand. Each evening since his arrival, he had taken his beach walk and thought about it all. Why Trill went away. Where was Daniel and what was he doing? And the war. The war and why he couldn't stop thinking about it. Why had he driven on an impulse three hundred miles south to this lonely island?

A few stars emerged above the moon. Trav vectored back toward the water's edge and forged further down the beach. The cool salt water lapped up to his knees and higher, to his faded, Bermuda shorts.

He turned to face the water and looked skyward, scanning newly visible stars. Another wave sloshed past him as he turned and headed northward . He had forgotten to turn a light on in the cottage, so there was no guidepost. He fretted that he had walked too far and suddenly felt a dull, hollow ache of aloneness. He wanted to be back at the cottage. He wanted to feel safe, or at least safer. And he wanted another drink. He stopped and took a deep breath.

*Trav, this is not a big problem. Look for the chimneys. The cottage is just up ahead or maybe behind.* Cloud cover had now lowered the visibility even further. *Which way?* He again scanned the lightless coast before and behind, then chose forward. It was ten minutes, maybe fifteen, when he stopped to look closely. He squinted a bit to be sure. *Yes, there it was.* A small boxy blackness ahead along the dune line. He walked further and saw the two protrusions on the roof line. His gait, now more steady, more relaxed, took him to his shadowy sanctuary.

Up the steps onto the sea-facing open porch, he reached and fumbled in the dark for the screen door handle. Stepping into the cottage, he fumbled again for the light switch, felt it on the wall, then headed for the kitchen and opened the refrigerator. He managed, in one hand, the bottle of chardonnay and, hooked around his index finger, a coffee mug. With the other hand, he carried a small battery-powered lamp, his journal and a ballpoint pen.

He was all set now, seated comfortably back on the porch. The little wooden side table held the wine bottle and the mug. The mug held a fulsome pour of chardonnay. His hand held the pen and the open journal. He drank some of the cool wine, looked down and wrote:

*August 25ᵗ, Nighttime*

He looked out beyond the small, battery-powered pool of light into the eastern darkness where the invisible sea gently ebbed and flowed. His listened to the small waves splash and run.

*It doesn't matter, Trav, what you write. Just whatever comes to your mind,* Dr. Ramos had said. *The important thing is to put something down. Anything. Write what comes to your mind. You need to write it and then read it the next day.*

Trav took in more wine, then looked down again at the journal. His pen touched the paper.

> *I am here on the island, staying at a very rustic old cottage on the beach. It's nighttime. Just had a nice walk. Got dark. Worried that I could not find my way back. This writing testifies that I did. Been here a couple of weeks now. It's ok, but I'm lonelier than I thought I would be. I like being by myself, but maybe not this much. A little bored maybe too. I think sometimes, especially at night like now, that I'm doing a stupid, irresponsible thing. But after Ashville, I just feel down, just so down, I wanted to do this. Martha was okay with it. Eryn too. Encouraged me, actually. She's back in school and it's good for her to try and focus again on that. Never could find Daniel. Goddamn him. He breaks my heart. Trill too. God, I miss her. Anger, fear, all rolled in together.'*

Trav stopped. Some more wine. Some more listening to the little waves. A gentle offshore breeze came in out of the darkness, rustling the pages of the notebook. Trav closed it, arched his back and threw his head back to receive the last of his cool elixir, and clicked off the lamp. He stood and went inside to bed.

Upstairs, he opened both bedroom windows, the east facing one and the south facing one. The breeze from the ocean flowed in, gently waving old, gossamer curtains. Trav turned out the light and lay on top of the covers, still in his damp khaki shorts and faded T-shirt. Through the beachside window, he could hear the rhythmic roll of the surf. Sleep came gently to him and it was a delicious, dreamless sleep enveloped in a friendly, nocturnal, salt-air breeze.

# CHAPTER 22

## *The Dinner Invitation*

Two seagulls on the beach were snapping and picking over the carcass of a crab. It was their cawing and clamoring that woke Trav. He swung his feet to the floor and sat up, peering out the east window to see the source of the screeching. Low scudding clouds hung along the horizon, blocking the sun that he estimated was already above the horizon.

Fishing today. That was his plan. Ann at the real estate office had told him there was a serviceable surf casting rod, net and tackle in the cottage and that he was free to use all the gear. Squid, he was told, was good bait for surf fishing, and he had bought a frozen package his first day on the island.

First, he would have his coffee and muffin and orange juice while journaling on the porch. His mouth was full of muffin. He chewed, swallowed, sipped his coffee, raised his dark glasses onto the crown of head and wrote:

*August 26th. Morning*

Trav looked to the beach. The seagulls had ended, or at least suspended, their battle and were calmly waddling around, looking for something else edible. The early morning sun, now above the cloud line, sparkled on the sea with such intensity that Trav had to look away and lower his dark glasses. *Fish wait for no man*, he thought He'd journal later.

Looking back at the paper, he wrote:

*I will journal after fishing. Promise!*

Leaving his coffee mug, notebook and pen out on the porch, wondering to himself if what he had written counted as journaling, he went inside to gather his gear. Out he came with an old ten-footer surf casting rod, net and tackle box into which he had placed his bag of squid. With the net and rod in one hand and tackle box in the other, he trudged down the steps onto the soft island sand and toward the ocean.

There was an incoming tide. He set up camp on dry sand and surveyed the beach. A glorious morning. How many beaches in America, he thought, are as empty as this in late August? Trav opened the small brown paper bag and laid the hunk of squid out to thaw. He then rummaged through the old tackle box for a sinker and hooks. The tackle was old, the hooks showing some rust. But it was, as Ann Sample had promised, serviceable.

He needed a knife to cut the bait. Back to the cottage and while he was at it, he filled his mug with orange juice and a little—just a little—vodka. He also grabbed a barely serviceable aluminum beach chair.

Back at camp, he sliced two strips of squid and laid them atop the tackle box. He sat in the rickety beach chair, adjusted his dark glasses and reached to the sand by the chair for his mug. The squid strips needed a little more time to thaw completely. He sipped his drink and took in the view. There was now not a cloud in the sky, not a ship nor boat visible on the water. Just the sweet empty vastness of the sea on a soft summer morning.

When the kids were young, he and Martha had taken a week's vacation at the beach in Nags Head. One day during that vacation, a day like this one, Trav and Daniel drove south across the Oregon Inlet bridge onto Hatteras Island and spent the better part of the day exploring. They fished that day too. Daniel was eight, maybe nine.

Trav had shown him how to cast, how to let the tackle sink to the sand under the water and how to keep just the lightest of tension on the line.

They caught no fish that day, but it didn't matter. Father and son were with one another and there was a quiet joy in the day. For Trav, the memory of that Hatteras outing years ago was now bittersweet. Had there been another person on the beach, he would have seen the faint, yet unmistakable hint of sadness in Trav's eyes. He thought of his son and dissected his state of mind. It was sadness and anger both. *Yes, both.* The loss of that day long gone. The sense of aloneness now breaking from underneath onto the surface. And also the other. The muscle's tensed now in his jaw and his neck.

*That rascal! Where the hell was he? Only thinks of himself.*

Trav reeled in and laid the big surf casting rod against the back of the aluminum chair. The hooked strips of squid swayed lazily at the top of the pole. He arched his back, stretching and scanning the beach and the sea.

*Think I'll give the blues a break for a while.*

He had walked south the previous night. Heading north this time, he wondered if he would see the man with the white hair. It was his first, maybe second, day on the island, while beach walking north that he had seen him. He was sitting on the sand just above the water line reading a book. He had waved as Trav approached, then stood. It was perhaps an unspoken island protocol that when you and another are the only two within sight on the beach that one stands and greets and chats.

"Morning," Trav had offered.

The white-haired man smiled up at him.

"And good morning to you."

From the neck down, the older gentleman looked quite shopworn, perhaps even a bit impoverished. Like Trav, he was sporting faded, threadbare khaki shorts. No belt. His T-shirt had a couple of dime-size holes in one sleeve. He was tanned and barefoot. Above the neck was the visage of different man altogether: a most distinguished-looking gentleman with an impressive set of fine, even white teeth, a ruddy but healthy complexion and a finely combed shock of thick grey hair.

Shaking hands, the man had removed his dark glasses to allow Trav to look directly into his clear brown eyes.

*He's the managing partner of an old-line law firm. Maybe a doctor. Maybe a university professor.*

"Hi, I'm Traveler McGale."

"Nice to meet you. Homer Wise."

They talked for a few minutes. Homer, gesturing to the sand at his feet and chuckling, offered, "Pull up a seat."

They had both eased onto the sand and sat facing the sea, their elbows resting on their knees. Homer, it turned out, was a very distinguished-looking car salesman. Actually, the longtime owner of a large dealership in Greenville, South Carolina. He was retired, but still owned the business, or at least part of it. He and his wife, Gwen, had been coming to Okracoke for many years, always renting 'their cottage' for the month of August, sometimes September too.

෨෧

This day, Trav plodded northward, knee deep in the surf, reviewing the unsettled state of his life. He could hardly bring himself to think about Trill and all that had happened and happened so quickly. It was his fault. Maybe she was going to die soon anyway, but if only he had driven her to the hospital that morning. He thought of Martha at home, arguing with himself yet again. He was being a selfish bastard to simply pack up and run to the beach, leaving her alone at home. No, it was not selfish. He had lost his twin sister and his life would simply never be the same. His son was nowhere to be found. He was an emotional Gordian Knot and he needed to get away, to decompress.

*I am not being selfish. Yes, you are. No, you're not.*

Trav's debate was interrupted by a wave that slammed him above the knees, almost knocking him over. He loped through the surf toward dry land, trying to right himself. Arriving at ankle depth water, he turned to his right and continued up the beach. In the distance was a small figure sitting on the sand. He walked on. He could now see it was Homer. Trav quickened his pace a bit, encouraged at the prospect of someone to talk with. He waved as he approached.

"Mornin', Homer."

Homer looked up from his newspaper.

"Well, hey there. How've you been?"

"Not bad."

Homer carefully folded his newspaper.

"Come sit a while."

They chatted about surface things, safe issues. Nice to have a beach to ourselves. Too bad summer is coming to an end. Fish were schooling out there earlier. And so on.

"Say," said Homer, "We're having an island friend over for supper tomorrow night. My wife is a pretty good cook and Sam's coming. You'll like Sam. Why don't you join us?"

"Well, I don't know," said Trav, pretending to be serious. "My schedule's pretty full tomorrow."

"Yeah, right." Homer laughed. "Six-thirty?"

"That's very nice of you," said Trav genuinely. "I'd love to."

# CHAPTER 23

## The Beach Dinner Party

He chuckled to himself as he stepped jauntily down off the cottage porch. *This,* he said to himself as his bare feet touched the soft sand*, is the new and improved Traveler at the Beach.* Showered, clean shaven, with his still wet hair neatly combed, he looked and felt like a different person. His clean, long sleeved, button down maroon shirt was tucked neatly into his khaki Bermuda shorts. He walked from the cottage to the water's edge and turned north, his Docksiders in one hand and his gift for the hosts, a bottle of white wine, in the other.

Homer had given him a detailed description of the mailbox by their cottage and which side of the road to pull over to and park. There were not many cottages up at that end of the beach and Trav was sure he wouldn't have any trouble getting there. Besides, Homer's directions didn't matter because he had decided to walk on the beach to the dinner party. Not really a party, he mused. Just Homer and his wife and Sam, whoever he is.

There was no wind. The sea was a placid, somnolent carpet of royal blue. The low dunes between the road and the beach cast lengthening shadows along the sand. As the sun descended, it began once more to move in on him. Light, almost imperceptible at first. Delicate tendrils. Then a stronger pull. His upbeat sense of 'I'm clean and dressed and steppin' out was being overtaken by a soft melancholy. A familiar melancholy. Trav had never talked to Martha or Trill or Spear or anyone about it. But he knew it and he had named it. It was his Sunset Sad.

127

He had come to realize that at times he welcomed the darkness, for it would mark the passing of Sunset Sad. He knew the feeling this day would pass, as it had all times before. He also knew that each barefoot step was bringing him closer to the company of others and a respite from the aloneness that pierced him now so deeply. He had arrived. Stepping up onto the beachside deck, he knocked on the screen door.

"Come on in," said Homer warmly.

Trav stepped into the pine paneled room as his host greeted him.

"I thought you were going to drive up."

"Well," said Trav, "it was such a beautiful evening, I decided to enjoy the walk. Here you go," he added, handing the wine to Homer.

"Thank you, my friend. You didn't have to do that."

Homer walked to a rustic sideboard and placed the wine next to an ice bucket. Trav heard the voices of two women in the kitchen.

"I think we've got things okay here," said one of the women. That was Homer's wife, he was pretty sure.

"Why don't you let me toss the salad?" said the other.

"Oh, we can do that a bit later. I think Homer's friend is here."

They emerged from the kitchen.

"Hello," said Trav.

Homer moved closer to the two women.

"Trav, you met Gwen the other day. And this is our old friend Samantha Brewer."

Trav shook the woman's hand as their eyes met. The mystery guest was definitely not Sam, the man. Fortyish, Trav guessed. Trim, athletic looking and very pretty. Her deep end-of-summer tan contrasted wonderfully with her ice blue eyes and short-cropped, light auburn hair. She looked down at Trav's feet, then said, "I see we both got the same invitation: 'Dinner at six-thirty, casual, no shoes.'"

Trav laughed, self-consciously holding his Docksiders in his hand.

"Right," he said, putting his shoes next to the screen door.

Hellos and nice-to meet-yous back and forth. Gwen absently wiped her hands on her apron.

"You all sit and relax. Dinner will be ready in a few minutes."

Drinks in hand Homer, Samantha and Trav sat in the big room.

"Sam has been coming to the island for, well, how many years?" said Homer.

"If I tell you how many years, Homer," she said, "I will be telling you my age. Let's just say practically since I was born."

"How long do you stay?" Trav asked.

"All summer long, I'm happy to say."

"All summer? Lucky you."

"I'm a teacher. So yes. All summer."

The cocktail hour chitchat proceeded. Trav learned that she was on the faculty at East Carolina University. She taught English and specialized in American literature. She liked Faulkner and Poe and Hemingway. Wallace Stegner was her favorite. Sam asked Trav about himself but received cryptic, guarded answers. He said he just came down 'for a while to sort things out.' She was considering whether to pursue the trail with more questions when they were interrupted.

"At last," Gwen called from the kitchen doorway, "our dinner is served."

Trav glanced around him, puzzled, seeing no dining room or a set dinner table.

"Let's eat," said Homer.

Trav stood, still puzzled, and padded barefoot, following his host. Homer held open the screen door for his guests. They stepped out onto the deck to behold a table set with four place settings of shrimp scampi, rice, and brussels sprouts. A nestle of small candles in the center of the table glowed magically in the summer twilight.

"Wow. Gwen," said Sam, "this looks absolutely wonderful!"

"Absolutely," said Trav. Then, turning to Samantha, he added, "I think we should put our shoes on, don't you?"

She laughed.

"I'm not driving home to get my shoes."

They sat. Homer held out his arms. The four of them held hands as he bowed his head and said a brief blessing. Then, raising his wine glass, he said, "Bon appetit."

"Bon appetit," they choroused.

It was during dessert—homemade peach pie ala mode—that Trav asked Sam, "So what do you do to fill up your days here all summer?"

He had caught her with a mouthful. She smiled closed-mouth and held up one finger. She swallowed.

"You mean besides tanning myself, walking on the beach and drinking fine wine?"

"Yes," said Trav. "Besides those things."

"Well, I do some writing. I write every day actually. And I sail."

It was the latter activity that piqued Trav's interest.

"You sail? What do you sail?"

"Small boats mostly," she said. "Sunfish, Hobies. I've got a Flying Scot, two actually. One that's hardly used."

"I love to sail," said Trav, remembering his days on the lake with Trill. He talked about his youth growing up around boats and spent a few minutes describing his sails on Lake Lure, describing everything in detail, everything except the sister who had been with him.

Sam, peach pie-on-fork suspended in front of her, said, "I've got that extra Flying Scot. It's not in the best shape in the world, but you're welcome to it while you're here."

"That's awfully nice of you," Trav said. "Sure."

The conversation was brought to a halt when Gwen rose to clear the table. Sam jumped to her feet to assist and the two ladies, arms full, headed inside and into the kitchen. Homer and Trav stayed and talked. An evening breeze had picked up. Homer leaned forward to blow out the candles. It was only a few minutes before the two ladies reemerged from the cottage.

"I'm going to say good night," said Samantha. She leaned into Gwen to give her a quick hug. "Thank you so much. It was delicious."

She turned to the men, but before she could said anything, Homer cut in.

"Trav, that wind is really kicking now. Why don't you let Sam drop you off?"

Samantha seemed momentarily caught off guard, but recovered quickly. She turned to Trav.

"Umm...absolutely. I'm going right by your cottage"

"I'm fine," said Trav. "I like the beach at night."

"Take the lift, man," said Homer. "You don't want to go all the way down there against the wind."

In fact, Trav was not relishing the long walk in the dark and decided rather quickly to protest no more.

Her car was a vintage black, stick-shift Jeep Wrangler with no side doors. Sam pushed her long legs down to the brake and clutch, geared into reverse, started her turn around and then stopped.

"I think you forgot your shoes." she said.

"Oh my gosh. Thanks. Be right back."

As they headed down island in the rickety open-air Jeep, Trav felt the sharp wind in his hair and was grateful not to be trudging along the dark surf.

"I'm up here on the left."

"I know. You're in the old Padgette house. My father was a good friend of the fellow who built it." She downshifted into second, then into first and pulled into the sandy hard pack, two-tracked path that led back to the cottage. She eased her Jeep up to the front door of the darkened cottage.

"There you go."

"I appreciate the ride," said Trav, reaching instinctively for the door handle that wasn't there.

Sam looked over at him. He could just barely make out her face in the dim glow of the instrument panel.

"By the way, I was serious about the Flying Scot. If you'd like to use it, you're more than welcome."

"Well," said Trav, hesitating, not sure how he should respond. "Actually, that would really be nice. But I don't want it to be any trouble for you."

Sam mused in mock seriousness.

"Let's see. I have a jam-packed schedule tomorrow, but between lying on the beach and procrastinating over writing, I might be able to squeeze in a delivery."

"A delivery?"

"Tomorrow, if the wind is right, I'll sail the boat up the beach. Then you can give me a lift back."

"Sounds good. Are you sure?"

"I'll try to get up here around four or five."

"Alright then," said Trav, hopping out of the jeep. "Thanks again."

As he pushed open the unlocked front door, Samantha called out to him.

"You forgot your shoes!"

He walked back to the Jeep and retrieved his Docksiders from her outstretched hand.

"Thanks again."

"You're welcome."

She smiled up at him.

"See you around cocktail hour."

"Bar will be open."

"Goodnight."

# CHAPTER 24

## *Arrival of the Flying Scot*

Two wine glasses sat poised on either side of a chilled, corked bottle of California chardonnay. A cereal bowl containing potato chips and a smaller bowl of salsa were also on the porch table. Trav glanced over at the wine, tempted to pour himself a glass. He was journaling, or at least attempting to, while repeatedly looking down the coast. He looked back at his opened notebook and wrote.

> *Had a good time at Homer and Gwen's last night. Samantha, nice lady from town, joined us.*

He looked up again, hoping to see a white sail coming into view. He removed his dark glasses and squinted. Nothing.

He looked down again at his journal, hoping for an interruption that would allow him not to write. Just write from the heart, Spear had advised. Don't think about it so much. Just let it flow.

He tapped his pen on the notebook. Then he started again.

> *I think this trip was a mistake. Trill is gone. Daniel is missing. Eryn is back in school, I hope doing okay. Why did I just abandon Martha the way I did? She said if I wanted to go off and decompress, it was alright. She didn't object. But was it selfish of me to get away? Shit. Wherever you go, there you are. Wanted to think about*

133

*the rest of my life without Trill. I could have saved her. I should have driven her to the chemo. Goddammit!! I should call Martha. I wonder if she has sent my mail down to the real estate office. Need to check.*

He looked over at the glistening droplets of cool water clinging to the side of the wine bottle.

*I'm adrift down here. Just goddamned adrift.*

He underlined the word adrift. Then he added:

*I want to go home.*

He closed his notebook, fastened the ballpoint pen to the top cover and looked up. There it was, a Flying Scot plying up the coast five hundred yards offshore. She was on a broad reach with her mainsail and small jib out on a starboard tack. Trav stood, walked to the railing of the porch and waved. He could see Sam clearly, one hand on the tiller while raising the other up high. He slipped off his shoes, adjusted his dark glasses, put on his hat and stepped down from the porch. Standing knee-deep in the light surf, he shoved his hands deep into the front pockets of his khaki shorts.

She was closer now and Trav could see her bronzed shoulders above her bathing suit, her dark glasses and blue Atlanta Braves baseball cap. She sailed just past the cottage, came about and luffed into the wind, allowing the boat to glide gradually into the beach. She was clearly a very seasoned sailor.

"Ahoy," Trav called out as he grabbed the bow to steady it.

"Ahoy to you, mate."

She raised the centerboard and hopped into the water. Each grabbed a starboard and port gunnel respectively and guided the Flying Scot through the small waves and onto the beach. They struggled, dragging the boat up twenty or thirty feet onto dry sand. Both were out of breath. They dropped the main and the small jib and left them bunched, cascading in loose, unruly folds on the boat.

Trav stood back and regarded the old boat. Looking up at the top of the mast, he commented, "She's really in pretty good shape."

Sam let her dark glasses hang from the strap around her neck and drop onto her upper chest.

"She is old, but she is a good boat. Sturdy. Sails are a lot newer than the hull."

Trav wiped his hands on the back of his pants.

"I've got some wine up on the porch."

"Great," said Sam, smiling. "I worked very hard to time my arrival to coincide with cocktail hour."

Seated on two rocking chairs, they clicked full glasses.

"Cheers."

Sam took a long slow sip of wine.

"Ahh, that hits the spot."

She took another, smaller sip and while looking straight out on the sea, said, "So, Mr. Traveler, tell me about the Mystery Man in the Padgette Cottage."

Trav looked over at her.

"Excuse me?"

"This is a very small island and everybody here knows everybody's business, or at least tries to. A good-looking man with a wedding ring on his left hand shows up at the end of the summer, rents a cottage with one day's notice, drives down the next day and moves in with no move out date."

Trav didn't answer.

"It's none of my business, of course. None. Just curious." Sam said.

"It's a long story."

Sam remained silent.

He balanced his wine glass on his knee and surveyed the far horizon, trying to decide what, if anything, he should say. He glanced over at Sam and realized he actually wanted to tell her his long story. He liked her and he felt comfortable with her. More importantly, he knew once he left the island he would never see her again, and so it mattered little what he shared with her. He felt safe.

"Well," he started, "I've had a troublesome time lately. Just some real blows. I told my wife I wanted to go to the beach to decompress a bit, to think things through."

"And how has that been working out for you so far?"

Trav took in a large swallow of wine and chuckled.

"I'm not sure real well so far."

"Because?"

"Because I get up in the morning and mess around. I fish. I take long walks on the beach. I eat. I have several happy hours throughout the day. I think. I told myself I wanted to sort things out down here. But I'm not even sure what that means, what I thought I wanted to accomplish. I'm just kind of drifting around in circles."

Sam looked over at him.

"You mentioned troublesome times." Sam paused. " Do you want to tell me about them?"

Trav took the wine bottle from the small table between them and held it out toward Sam.

"A touch more?"

Sam held her glass under the bottle. He refilled her glass, then his own and settled back into the old wicker rocking chair.

"Yes, I guess I would like to tell you. Why not?"

He paused and looked again at the beach, Sam's boat and at the sea.

"For starters, we have a seventeen—eighteen now—year-old son who's a drug addict."

"I'm sorry."

"Yeah, he's been a real handful all his life. Smart kid, but rebellious."

Trav told Sam all about their challenges with Daniel, the incident of the flying chair, Maine, jail, entering rehab, the runaways and Daniel's disappearance. All of it.

Sam took a sip of her wine.

"So where is he now?"

"We have no idea, really. We haven't heard from him since the twenty-eighth of June. My guess is he's hanging out with some druggies in Maine somewhere. But that's just a guess."

Trav talked on. The shadows lengthened along the sand dunes. A light afternoon breeze wafted in from the north. He told Sam about Triil, about her cancer and the car accident, and about the funeral in

Ashville. He talked about Martha and what a good wife and mother she was and how all this had been so hard on her and how he was feeling guilty that he had run off to the beach, leaving her to manage things at home.

"Have you talked to your wife since you've been down here?"

"Once. A couple of days after I got here. I told her before I left I wanted to be pretty much incommunicado down here. I've left my cell phone off. Martha understood. Said she would call the real estate office if there were something urgent. Also said she would send any important mail to A Place at the Beach."

Trav stopped his story. He took a deep breath, feeling good, but feeling a bit worn from suddenly divulging large emotional chunks of his life. Sam, seeming to recognize his need for a respite, remained quiet. Together, they watched the sea turning from blue to black and the breeze carving ripples into the surface. Finally, Trav broke the silence.

"Want some more wine?"

"Oh, no thanks. I think I've had plenty."

Silence again.

Then sam asked, "What sort of work did you go into after college?"

Trav laughed.

"Why is that funny?"

"Well, it was a kind of work, for sure. It's just the way you asked that struck me as odd."

"So what then?

"Right after college, I spent two years in Vietnam. Marine Corps."

"Oh, I see," she said, then added awkwardly, "I guess I should say thank you for your service."

Trav's eyes fixed on some distant point out to sea.

"Thank you," he said softly. "But I've always hated it when people say that to me."

Sam turned to face him.

"Why? It's a compliment."

"I know it's a compliment, but it's just that...it was such a screwed up war. I mean really. The compliment, I know it's always well-meaning when folks say it, but it makes it sound like it was some sort of noble endeavor. It never seemed very noble to me."

"I can appreciate that, but you went over there. You did what you were asked to do and you did your best."

Trav didn't respond. He sat quietly again, swirling the last of his wine. He put his glass on the table, grabbed the empty bottle, stood and went into the cottage to fetch more. Back out on the deck. he gestured in her direction with the new bottle.

"Sure you don't want a touch?"

"No, no. Actually, I should be getting back."

Trav sat back down. They had agreed the day before that Sam would sail to the cottage and Trav would drive her home. Except for the psychiatrist at the VA, Trav had not talked to anyone about Vietnam in a long time, and something in him wanted to revisit 'that day.' He looked over at her in the fading evening light.

"Can you stay just another minute? I just wanted to..."

Sam hesitated. "I guess."

"Thank you."

Trav filled his own glass. She glanced over at him and saw his vacant, unblinking stare. She knew he was no longer on the deck of a cottage on Okracoke Island. He was back there. Patience was one of Sam's leading virtues. She let him be. He would talk when he was ready. But for the rhythmic cascading of waves along the shoreline, there was no sound. Finally, he started.

"Vietnam was a long time ago, but pieces of it are like yesterday. There was this one night. It's like a movie clip that gets played again and again. Stuck in rewind."

"What's the clip about?"

"It's about May 14, 1968."

Trav talked on and on. He told her about his company, about Vietnam's central highlands and about his Marine Corps friends. He told her about Vince and about the night he died and about his own futile, frantic efforts to save him. He also told her about the helicopter crash. Trav brought his monologue to a close. He leaned his head back, looked at the ceiling and closed his eyes.

"Maybe you didn't want to hear all that. If so, I'm sorry."

"It's quite alright, "I can appreciate what you went through."

Trav opened his eyes and turned toward her.

138

"Can you?" he asked sharply.

Sam broke his gaze and turned away from him.

"I think so. My father was killed in Vietnam. I was fourteen."

Trav rolled back and stared at the ceiling.

"Oh Jesus. Oh, I'm sorry, Sam."

"It's alright. It's okay. I'm glad you told me what you did. For good or ill, we have that bloody war in common."

It was now almost dark. The twilight breeze was no more. They sat in the still silence of the coming night. Trav drained his glass.

"I've kept you too long. Let's get you home."

"Okay."

She stood and peered into darkness toward the beach.

"The tide's coming in. We should move the boat further up."

"Right."

Trav stood unsteadily and followed her down the deck steps and out onto the cool, dry sand. They each grabbed the sloop at the gunnels, dragged her up against a dune and then walked back around to the front of the cottage to Trav's car.

"Are you sure you're okay to drive?"

"Huh?"

"All the wine. Can you drive?"

"Oh, sure."

He fumbled through his pockets for his keys, managed to find them, start the car and head it in the direction of the village.

"By the way," she said, not taking her eyes off the road, "I have some mail for you at the house."

"Mail?"

"My friend, Ann, at the real estate office gave it to me to give to you."

"Gave it to you?"

"I told you, this is a very small town, my friend. "Everybody knows everybody's business."

She directed Trav to her house and asked him to pull up by the front door.

"Wait here. I'll be right back."

She opened the unlocked front door, stepped in, then out again and walked around to Trav's side of the car.

"Here you go," she said, handing him a single, large padded envelope.

"Thanks," Trav replied, looking up at her, "and thanks for lending me the boat. I'll take good care of her."

"Enjoy it."

Sam put the envelope down next to him.

"Sam, I'm sorry I talked about the war. I didn't mean to...And I am sorry about your father. I hope I didn't..."

She interjected gently.

"Trav, I said it was okay. Please don't think a thing about it. Drive safely and get some sleep."

# CHAPTER 25

## The Mail

The morning sun, high and bright, filled the bedroom. Trav, still fully clothed, lay in a fetal position on the bed. The night before, he had managed to return to the cottage without incident, although he would have only a fuzzy recollection of the drive back. Outside the window, gulls were again squabbling loudly over a morsel of sand crab. Trav stirred and rolled over. He opened his eyes, surveyed his surroundings and then closed them again. A gull screeched. Trav sat up and looked out the window.

*What am I going to do today? What did I do yesterday?*

Out on the deck, he sipped his coffee, staring discontentedly at the sea, hoping his headache would go away. There was something, something he was going to do today. *What was it?* He drank more coffee and took a bite of banana, trying to recollect the events of the previous day. Sam. The boat. Their talk. He drove her home.

He peeled the remainder of his banana and took another bite. He must have driven back here. *The mail. That was it.* What had he done with that package of mail?

He went into the cottage, looked around the living room and the kitchen. Then he realized it was probably in the car. Sure enough.

Back on the porch with a fresh mug of coffee, he opened the padded mailer. On a yellow post-it stuck to the top envelope, was a handwritten note from Martha:

*Here is some mail that I thought you would want to see.*
*Be well. Come home soon. I love you. M*

The post-t was affixed to a letter from Eryn:

*Dear Mom,*
*Having a good time here. Jenny's parents are real*
*nice. Boy, you are right: Nantucket is a way cool place!!*
*Loving it, but sort of starting to want to get back to school.*
*Won't be long now!!!*
*I still think about Aunt Trill all the time. So sad. I'm*
*worried about Dad just heading off to that island all*
*by himself. Weird. Tell him I love him. Any news from*
*Daniel?*
*See you in a week.*

*Love, Eryn*

Trav reread the letter, then slipped it back in its envelope. He was so proud of Eryn and he marveled at how she, like her mother, could love and care for him so freely, so openly. He looked again out to sea, out to the far horizon. *I should go home.*

There were eight more letters, all expressions of condolence over the loss of Trill. He read them quickly and shoved them back into the large mailer. There was one more. Trav held it in both hands and regarded the envelope for a long time. The addressee, Mr. Traveler S. McGale, was typed. The return address in the upper left hand corner read:

*Records Department*
*Presbyterian Memorial Hospital*
*19704 Longview Road*
*Charlotte, North Carolina*

He opened the envelope. It contained a short form letter stating that his requested medical records were enclosed. Behind the letter were two sheets. The first was a photocopy of faded but legible handwriting.

*Record of Birth*

*September 22, 1946. Male NFN McGale. Live birth. Weight 5 lbs. 1 oz. Umbilical cord wrapped. Blue baby. Severe loss of oxygen. Status: Grave. Immediate divert incubator.*

*Under the heading Remarks, the barely legible handwriting read: One of triplets. Healthy female, stillborn male and subject NFN McGale male.*

The second form, also a faded photocopy, read:

*Record of Discharge*

*December 3, 1946 Traveler Syms McGale. Weight: 6 lbs. 15 oz. Physical health: fair. Mental: Unknown. Will need testing/follow-up. Discharged to parents.*

The signature of both forms was equally faded and equally illegible. Trav looked up and then up further into the sky.
*Triplets? Blue baby. Grave? In an incubator until December? Jesus.*
He took a deep breath, struggling to take in what he had just read. He read the forms a second time, then a third. He went inside, tossed the mail on the old wooden table in the living room and wandered into the kitchen. He took a deep breath and reached for his bottle of vodka. *Time for a screwdriver.*
Trav, tall glass in hand, resumed his usual position on the rocking chair out on the deck. He gazed at the sparkling, late summer day.
*I would have had a brother. I did have a brother.*
A small sandpiper scampered along the crest of the dunes. The vodka and orange juice tasted great. He chuckled, remembering the old W. C. Fields line: "Everyone has to believe in something. I believe I'll have another drink." Then he stopped chuckling. He needed to do something worthwhile today. He reached for his journal notebook, opened it and started to write:

*August 27ᵗʰ. Still at the beach. Thinking I shouldn't be just spinning my wheels down here. Martha sent mail. Got the report from the hospital in Charlotte. It confirmed in more detail what Mother had told me. But also we were triplets! A brother...almost. God! Reading the reports I felt...*

Trav paused. He put the back end of the pen between his teeth. He looked down at what he had written, reading the words. He felt...what? A loneliness. It felt like...He started to write again.

*I felt like I was in a void. Hollow. Back in the incubator? Not a good feeling.*

Trav closed the notebook and turned his attention back to his drink. Morning sunlight danced out on the water. Birds were circling and diving out beyond the surf. There must be fish out there, he thought as he went back into the cottage and came out laden with the large casting rod, tackle, bait...and a cold beer.

His first cast was a beauty. The baited hooks and pyramidal lead weight soared high and far before plunging far out beyond the surf. He settled in to wait, as all fishermen wait, for 'the big one.' His mind drifted. *Blue baby. The other boy, poor little devil.* He reeled in a bit, putting a light tension on his line and took a swallow of the beer he had thoughtfully brought down to the beach with him. *Incubator... three months?* He squinted into the bright sunshine. *Maybe I shouldn't have written to the hospital. What purpose did it...*

"Whoa, Nelly!" he said out loud.

Above his head, the end of the rod was bowed in an arc and dancing with 'fish on.' Trav leapt to his feet and began to reel in as he waded into the surf.

His catch was a good one. A bluefish, three pounds, he guessed. Triumphantly, he lugged his prize, his gear and his empty beer bottle back to the cottage. He stowed his gear, put the big blue in the refrigerator and drifted through the next few hours. A long walk south on the beach. A late lunch consisting of crackers, some cheese and an apple. Then an afternoon nap.

Later in the afternoon, a breeze sprang from the northeast. Light, but steady.

*A sail? Yes, indeed. Capital idea. An afternoon sail.*

Trav, pleased with his morning's success and now happy to have something concrete to do, bounded onto the beach and raised the sails on Sam's Flying Scot. Sliding the rudder into its bracket, he noticed the odd name on the stern, affixed with black, stick-on letters: B RACE ONE. *An odd name for sure.* He swung the bow around toward the water and dragged the sloop into the surf. Thigh deep in the water, he clambered aboard, grabbed the tiller in one hand and the main sheet in the other and glided out to sea. The wind freshened, the boat heeled slightly and picked up speed.

He felt good. He felt better than good. Wonderful it was to feel the pull of the tiller in his hand and to look skyward and to see the gleaming, taut mainsail overhead. It felt good to put some distance between himself and land and to be in motion. The destination was irrelevant. It was the sensation of energy and forward motion that was all. As Trav trimmed the sails, the Flying Scot heeled more to port and her bow cut smartly through the rolling waves. He pulled on the main sheet and impulsively said out loud, "Come on, baby. Let's ride!"

For the first time since coming to the island, he felt truly happy. He looked to his left, back toward the coast. The water was a dancing carpet of sparkling diamonds. He remembered those same diamonds on Lake Lure, where they had shimmered and shined in the same way. Out on the lake that day, Trill had said it was God's pathway to heaven. Trav closed his eyes, sailing B RACE ONE purely by feel and seeing Trill. He saw her college-age when she was her most beautiful. Her summer tan, the cute freckles, just like Eryn's, under her eyes, her warm smile. The twins never actually sailed together at that age, but Trav saw her nevertheless at twenty on a sailboat with him on the lake. She looked at him and laughed her wonderful laugh.

When he opened his eyes, the Flying Scot had swung around into the wind and was about to luff. He pulled the tiller and course corrected. Against his long-held skeptical outlook on life and the afterlife, he looked to the heavens.

*I hope you're up there, baby. I love ya.*

He sailed on happily, not wanting the day to end. He was now far offshore and had to search the distant coastline to spot his cottage. The sun was gliding lower in the western sky. He pushed the tiller to starboard and headed for home. It was a wonderful sail. A most wonderful day.

⌘

That evening, back on terra firma, Trav glanced out the small kitchen window at the dimming twilight. Leaning forward and looking hard to his left, he could just make out Race One's silhouette safely hauled hard up against the sand dunes. He looked down with pride at his catch of the day. The bluefish, head and tail still on, had been gutted and scaled and lay before him by the sink on a metal tray. Trav lathered the fish with butter. He then took a long swig from his open bottle of chardonnay and liberally splashed the rest over the fish.

"There," he said out loud, sliding his catch into the oven.

On the porch, he sat, knees together cradling the large plate. He picked a bone from the fish. *Nothing better. An afternoon on the water. A freshly caught blue and a bottle of vino.* He ate his fill, then stood and threw the uneaten remains of his meal onto the dunes. He sat back down, caressing the wine bottle between his hands, then went back in the cottage and returned to the porch with old man Padgette's battery-powered lamp, his journal notebook and his pen. He sat for a long time, a very long time, gazing into the darkness. Finally, he took a long draw from the bottle, opened his notebook and began to write.

*August whatever.*

*Had my best day since coming here. Caught my dinner. Sailed this afternoon on Sam's boat way offshore.. Trill was with me, I felt. It was an afternoon.*

Spear said 'Don't look for the perfect words. Just let it flow. Trav continued to write.'

> *It was an afternoon like...like what? Like floating almost. A lightness. A delicious, wonderful lightness of being. Just finished my blue. Also delicious. Found out I was one sick puppy coming into this old world. Found out I had a brother. Parents never told me. What the hell?*

Trav reached over to his 'companion' in a bottle. He held it by the neck, but did not pick it up. He looked down at the page illuminated by the soft glow of the little lamp. Then, oddly, his pen seemingly disconnected from his hand, began again.

> *"It is about loss. I'm starting to see it now. It's about a feeling of emptiness. Being robbed. Spear—I get it now— hinted at it, but I didn't understand. Dad wasn't around. His body was there – sometimes too much. But not for me. I would be ten feet away and would be missing him. Vince dying in my arms. I couldn't save him. Gone that night. Living nightmare. Daniel gone too. Can't save him either. Trill gone and I should have...I've got Martha and Eryn. Thank God for them."*

Trav put down the pen and reached once more for the bottle. This time he craned his head and let the cool wine flow into him. His pen resumed.

> *"Yes. Thankful for M and E. But what kind of a god operates this way? I'm not that bad a person. Maybe I am. No, I'm not, damn it! It's not fair. Why did you take them? Them and not me?"*

"You can't figure it out, Trav," Spear had told him on more than one occasion. "You just need to be in life and flow with it," he would say.

*Need to be in life? What the hell does that mean? I don't get you, god. Sorry, My Man, I just don't get you."*

Trav slapped the notebook closed, drank the last of the wine in a large gulp, threw the bottle out over the dunes and staggered to bed.

❧❦

Upstairs, another cool offshore breeze flowed in through the bedroom window. Trav fell quickly into a deep sleep. The wind became stronger and colder. He reached for a blanket that wasn't there. He curled into himself to gather a spot of warmth and slid into a dream where he pressed himself hard against the muddy hill as enemy gunfire flew close overhead. Vince was out in front of him, exposed, wounded and crying out. Daniel, lying flat against the mud next to his father, leapt up and ran into the enemy fire toward him.

"No!" Trav screamed. "Get back!"

But Daniel ignored him and ran on into the blackness of the night. Then the dream changed. Trav and his sister were in their childhood home arguing about something. He couldn't piece together what the dispute was about, but heard himself saying, "Go ahead then if that's what you want to do. You're like Dad. Just as stubborn as a mule." Trill stormed out of the old house, saying as she slammed the door behind her, "I'm going to drive myself, goddamnit!"

The scene changed again. Martha took Trav by the arm.

"I'll drive, honey. You just sit and relax. It'll be fine."

Trav felt unsure, lost.

"Here's your coat," Martha said.

Trav dutifully climbed into the passenger side of their car. Martha started the engine, turned over her shoulder to see behind her and backed out of the driveway.

She looked over at her husband and said, "Put your seat belt on now."

"Where are we going?"

Martha reached up to adjust the rear view mirror.

"Gotta get a clear sight of where we've been."

"Where are we going?"

"Charlotte," she said, seeing that Trav was confused. "You said you wanted to go to Charlotte, didn't you?"

Trav awoke. He was cold. He closed the window, slid under the sheet and fell back into a fitful, dreamless sleep.

# CHAPTER 26

## Second Sail

The next morning was a carbon copy of the previous one. The same cloudless blue sky. The same squabbling gulls. Out to sea, the same sparkling path to heaven. Trav sipped his coffee out on the deck, replaying the tape of the previous happy day: the hospital report, then the morning success fishing, the delicious baked blue and most of all, the glorious afternoon sail. He closed his eyes, trying to recapture the joy he felt out there. It was, indeed, a good day and he would simply replicate it.

*It worked yesterday, it will work today.*

He would have a second good day. Then he would go home.

Down on the beach, he baited his hooks, checked his reel and waded into the gentle surf. Slowly, he positioned the big rod behind him. Then, with a smooth sweeping motion, he swung the pole over his head, letting the tackle soar on its flight eastward, splashing far out into the cool, blue-green ocean. If today was to be like yesterday, Trav thought, a large Blue should be tugging in short order. But this day, for some reason, was deciding to veer in a different direction.

He fished for an hour, checking his bait from time to time, periodically hooking on fresh squid. No bites. All morning long. No bites. It would be a different day, a very different day. He gave up on the fishing. Back in the cottage, he made himself a ham and cheese sandwich that he consumed along with a cold beer. Actually, two cold beers.

He took a walk up the beach, then succumbed to the pull of an afternoon nap. He awoke refreshed and looked out the second story window to check the sailing conditions. There was a breeze out of the southwest. It was light, but enough to move B Race One along nicely.

Back once again on the beach, he raised the sails and dragged the boat down to the water's edge. A line of low cumulus clouds hung along the western horizon. Over the ocean, the sky was blue and clear. Trav hauled the sloop out into the light surf and pushed the rudder into the down position.

*This part of yesterday I will replicate.*

He scrambled aboard and grabbed the tiller and main sheet. The flapping sails filled with wind and became taut as Race One heeled over, cutting smartly through the light chop out to sea on a broad reach. Trav, craning his neck to admire the bulbous white main set against a cerulean sky, smiled. He pushed the faded varnished tiller to starboard, causing the boat to fall away to port and run downwind on a northeasterly course. He headed up along the beach, angling further out to sea. As the strengthening wind powered him forward, his lingering sadness over Trill, his worries about his son and his discomfort over the hospital report all fractured and splintered and fell away into the wake behind him.

Waves slapped happily against the hull and splashed a bit up onto Trav's legs. Like a violinist or an athlete 'in the zone,' Trav, for the first time in recent memory, felt a smooth flow, synchronized with the universe. The afternoon light started its subtle shift from yellow-white to gold. Trav and Race One, his newfound friend, sailed on. A half-hour, maybe forty minutes, passed.

Then there was something. The wind was cooler now. Trav sensed the something. It was...it was...a feeling. The flow was broken. Something. He turned and looked astern.

"Oh, shit!," he said out loud. He dropped his sunglasses, allowing them to hang from the strap around his neck and stared at the coastline behind him. *Oh* God! The far sky was a menacing wall of black. To the south, white caps ripped along in jagged rows. Trav, a seasoned sailor, knew exactly what he was seeing: A Carolina summer squall. Localized, compact. In an hour, it would blow through and the sun would again be shining. But in the meantime, it would be dark, dangerous and deadly.

His cottage behind him was already hidden in the blackness. To run back there would be to head directly into the teeth of the storm. Trav knew in an instant his choice—and his only chance. He would jibe, then angle to the northwest and up toward the coast. Maybe, just maybe, he could get to the beach before the storm got to him. He changed course, brought the boom around and trimmed both sails. The race was on.

Trav looked around the boat. He had set sail barefoot, wearing khaki shorts, a faded green T-shirt, a white baseball cap and dark glasses. No life jacket. No anchor. No life ring. *What an idiot. What a fucking idiot! You know better, Traveler. What were you thinking?* He concluded that, basically, he hadn't been thinking much of anything, except how nice it would be to sail.

He took a quick look back over his left shoulder and turned more to starboard and away from the weather, hoping to outrun the squall. The race was on, indeed, but Trav, looking down the coast, knew it was a race he would not win. A whitecapped wave crested over the side of the boat, sloshing green water into the bottom of the cockpit. Trav thought of Martha and Eryn. He thought of Daniel. He saw the three of them standing at a gravesite saying goodbye to him. He looked up fearfully at his mainsail straining against the high wind.

"Please God," he said out loud, "I really need you just now. Please, My Man!"

Far to the north, there was still blue sky, but the inexorable march of the storm now covered the sun. Rain came and flew almost horizontally into Trav's face. He looked westward, trying to estimate his distance to the beach. Suddenly there was a blinding flash of light and a cannon shot. The shock of the lightning strike—so close, so imminent—threw him down onto the floorboards of the open cockpit. He scrambled upright just in time to reach the tiller and prevent a capsizing. Drenched now, he looked again toward the beach. Six hundred, maybe seven hundred yards, he guessed.

The heart of the storm then closed in around him and the beach disappeared. Through the darkness and driving rain, he could barely see the bow of the sloop. Another flash, another cannon shot. The wind roared to gale force, pushing Race One far over. The seas were on the verge of pouring into the cockpit. Trav reacted instinctively, pointing the bow to port, hoping to head into the wind, to luff the sails and to stabilize the boat. His instinct, that of a seasoned sailor, was the right one, but his reaction became an overreaction. Race One's bow now swung wildly. The boom snapped around overhead and slammed violently onto the port side.

There was another cannon shot, his one actually a small rifle shot. It was not lightning this time, but the sound of the mast snapping. In an instant, struggle turned to calamity. Trav looked up just in time for the careening mast to hit his forehead. The darkness became total. The din faded to silence. The shock of his fall into the cold sea brought him back to consciousness.

*Underwater...need air. This is it...this is...*

Then came a terrible yank on his left arm and excruciating pain in his shoulder. Prior to the calamity, back five minutes before when there was some hope, he had wrapped the sheet several times around his wrist. The now capsized, floundering sloop was lifted by a wave and tugged Trav, like a heavy sea anchor, astern. The line had pulled Trav to the surface. He reached for the line with his right hand and disentangled his left. Race One wallowed and bobbed with the waves, half sunken, half afloat.

Trav managed to pull himself to the boat and hook an elbow over the floating mast, gasping for air, feeling—fearing—he might fall back into unconsciousness. *Don't take me yet, My Man. Please.* He rested his head on the mast. He drifted with the tangled mass of hull and lines and sails. Waves washed over him. His arms, the good one crooked over the mast and his injured one, both ached. His grip on the mast was slipping. *Not much longer.*

He closed his eyes and prayed again to the god he was never sure was there, the god he often doubted cared a wit about him even if he were there. His grip slipped further. He rested his head against the hull of the sloop and closed his eyes. *Please, God. Please let me...*He was distracted when his foot hit something. Then his other foot bumped onto something. *What?* A cresting wave lifted him and the tangled rig up and forward then down into a trough. Both feet hit at once this time, touching...sand. Sand! Trav was walking on sand below the water!

The waves of the breaking surf washed the stricken sloop and her desperate helmsman ashore. Trav, too spent to stand, remained motionless on his hands and knees as the dark, foamy water rushed past him, receded, then again swirled around his legs and hands. He crawled, left shoulder in searing pain, up onto the beach past the surf line and rolled onto his back. He touched his hand to his throbbing forehead and felt a gash above his brow. He sensed the blood on his face and his hand. He closed his eyes and let the rain pour down on him and slipped into unconsciousness.

It was quiet save for the splashing sound of the surf rolling on shore. Trav opened his eyes. Still on his back, looking straight up, he saw only a cloudless blue. *Daytime?* He struggled to sit up. His head and shoulder throbbed. He looked down, seeing for the first time raw, bloody scrapes on both shins. Behind him he glimpsed the sun low in the sky above a row of scrub pines. He turned back to the ocean to look at the wreckage before him.

It was a mess, but it was still Sam's boat. Hoping in a hazy, confused way to save the sloop for her, he struggled over and, with his one good hand, grabbed the bow and pulled. He managed to slide her a few feet further onto the beach before falling exhausted onto the sand. He again rolled onto his back, breathing hard.

*What do I do now?*

Then he groaned and shouted out loud, "What the fuck do I do?"

He knew there was only one thing to do. He would rest, then walk south on the beach and try to reach his cottage. Fortunately, aside from the badly scraped shins, his legs were functional. He rested, then headed down the beach. He couldn't see his cottage. He couldn't see any cottage. He walked on as the beach curved slightly inland. The sun would set in a few minutes.

He looked ahead. There it was, the boxy shape with the double chimney. Trav started to feel faint. He looked again toward his goal.

*There it was. Wait. What?*

He stared at the cottage. He was sure the porch light just went on. Someone stepped off the porch onto the beach.

*Maybe it wasn't his cottage...but the double chimney? Yes, it had to be his.*

The person on the beach looked up in Trav's direction. The man took a step forward, then stood motionless, looking, peering up the coast at him. Trav continued to walk and could now see that the man was a woman and she began to walk, then jog toward him.

"Trav? Trav, is that you?"

Trav waved and managed a hoarse, "Yeah. Yeah, it's me."

He tried to run, then fell. As Sam reached him, Trav rolled onto his back for the third time. She knelt by him and seeing his forehead, gasped.

"Oh, my God!" She helped him to his feet and together they made their way to the cottage.

Trav wanted her to get him into his bed in the cottage, but she would have none of it. Too weak to put up much resistance, he gingerly maneuvered himself into the passenger seat of Sam's Jeep. She backed out onto the road and roared toward town.

The doctor on duty at the clinic put twenty-seven stitches in his forehead, treated and bandaged both legs, realigned his dislocated shoulder, put his arm in a sling and gave him a vial containing some large pills.

Riding away from the clinic with Sam, Trav was lost in thought.

*How could this day have gone so wrong? How could I have been so stupid?*

He sensed that Sam wanted to talk, but she held her tongue. Reaching a four-way stop intersection, she turned toward town. Trav looked over at her.

"Where are you going?"

"My house," Sam said, keeping her eyes straight on the road. "You are in no condition to be alone."

Trav started to protest.

"No, Really, I'll be fine."

"Trav, don't argue with me," she said with a distinct edge to her voice. "Just don't."

Wisely, he didn't.

☙❧

In her living room, Sam got him settled on the couch. "Do you want something to eat?" she asked, her tone this time softer.

"Well, maybe," Trav said. "I'm not too hungry."

Then he added, "Sure. Anything." He looked up at her.

"Do you by any chance have any whiskey? Bourbon maybe?"

Sam looked at him, hesitated, then said, "Sure. Let me see what I can rustle up," as she disappeared into her kitchen. She returned with a ham and cheese sandwich and chips on a plate and a large tumbler. Bourbon on the rocks.

"Here you are."

"Thanks," was all Trav could muster.

She disappeared again into the kitchen and reappeared with her own sandwich and a glass of ice tea. She sat in her big easy chair across the room from Trav and raised her glass to him.

"Cheers," she said without cheer.

"Cheers."

"So," said Sam, "would you like to tell me about your adventure on the high seas?"

Trav was chewing. He swallowed, then reached for the bourbon with his one unencumbered hand.

"Sure," he said finally looking over at her. "First, though, I want to tell you how sorry I am about the Flying Scot. I really feel bad about it. You were so nice to let me use it and I..."

"Oh, please," Sam interrupted. "It's just a boat, an old one at that. You are very lucky to be alive, my friend. Don't worry about the boat."

He looked down at his bandaged shins and bare feet.

"God, I was such an idiot. I know better. No life jacket. Didn't pay attention." His voice drifted off.

Sam sipped her tea, regarding her wounded charge.

"Tell me what happened."

He told her the whole story: The glorious southwest breeze, his joy on the broad reach and the downwind run off to the northwest, the storm, the wind, the lightning and his race against the squall, and the final catastrophe.

"That's it," he said finally. "That's what happened."

Sam finished the last of her wine.

"And you're right."

"Right about what?" Trav asked.

"You are an idiot."

They both laughed.

"Now," Sam said standing up, "you are going to bed."

She settled Trav, who put up no argument, in the larger bed in her bedroom and put herself in a single bed in the guest room.

# CHAPTER 27

## Missing Letters

Trav awoke the next morning to the smell of fresh coffee and sizzling sausage. He rolled to his left, forgetting about his shoulder and the sling. He winced and groaned but managed to crawl out of bed still clad in his khaki shorts and his blood-stained T-shirt. He stood in the doorway to the kitchen, trying not to stare too long at Sam's physique as she faced away from him, tending frying sausage.

"Morning," he said.

She turned with a jerk, her spatula raised in defense.

"Oh, you scared me. Good morning to you. How did you sleep?"

"Okay, I guess. Except for periodic painful wake-up calls from my shins and my head and my shoulder, fine."

"Have a seat." Sam pointed with her spatula at her small kitchen table. "Breakfast is comin' right up."

After breakfast, she drove him back to his cottage. She pulled into his drive, shifted the Jeep into neutral and looked over at him with a stern expression.

"You take it easy now. I mean it. I've got things to do today, but I'll stop by later this afternoon to check on you."

"Okay," Trav said. He fumbled to find the latch to the passenger side door that still wasn't there and stepped out. He turned back and leaned his head into the open window.

"Sam, I can't thank you enough for taking care of me like this. Seriously. I would be a mess without you."

Sam looked at him.

"I hate to break this to you, Mister, but you're a mess even with me around."

Trav smiled and tapped the roof of the Jeep .

"You're right about that. Thanks again."

Sam shifted into reverse.

"I'll see you this afternoon."

Trav haltingly, gingerly maneuvered himself up the front steps and into the cottage. On the drive back with Sam, he had made his plan for the rest of the morning.

*A Screwdriver. A stiff one. Maybe two. Then lie down.*

Late in the afternoon, after successfully executing his plan for the day, he was sitting on the back deck enjoying his view of a calm Atlantic. It was almost five o'clock, when he heard the crunch of tires pulling up in front of the cottage. He heard her turn off the engine. Sam walked around the south side of the cottage and saw Trav in his usual perch.

"Hey."

"Hey to you."

She climbed the four steps onto the porch and sat beside him.

"How are you feeling?"

"Pretty sore," Trav said. "But all in all, not too bad."

"Did you take those pain pills?"

"I did," he lied, not wanting to share the fact that he opted for the painkilling effects of vodka and orange juice.

"Well, I just wanted to make sure you're okay and that you weren't doing anything…anything else…stupid."

Trav laughed, looked over at her and replied, "As you know by now, I'm sure, I am always capable of that." Then he added off-handedly, "How 'bout a drink?"

"Do you have juice or a coke or something?"

"Orange juice."

"Sure."

"I can turn that orange juice into a nice screwdriver."

"Just O.J. for me."

"Okay. Be right back."

Sitting alone on the deck, Sam noticed an envelope sitting on the table. She picked it up. A letter from a hospital in Charlotte. She looked around to sense if Trav was still busy in the kitchen. Then she quietly slid the letter out of the envelope, read it and placed it carefully back on the table.

"Here you go," said Trav, back on the deck, handing Sam her juice and holding on to his own fortified drink. They chatted and sipped and took in the warmth of the summer afternoon. They sat in silence for a few moments. Trav then said, "I don't know if this would interest you, but how about a walk up the beach to take a look at your boat?"

Sam expressed some surprise, then after a moment's reflection, said, "Well, alright. Why not?" Then she added, "Are you sure you're up to it?"

Trav was already on his way down the steps to the beach. "I'm sure," he said over his shoulder.

They walked shoeless at the edge of the surf. Rounding the curve in the beach, Trav raised his right hand and pointed. "There she is."

Sam looked at the amorphous mass at the water's edge a quarter of a mile ahead. Reaching the boat, she insisted Trav sit and rest, which he did without objection. Looking at B Race One, he mused, "It's a bit hard for me to look at today."

"Well," said Sam, "it's not the prettiest of sights. Not as awful, though, as I thought it would be. Mast is shot, but it looks like the hull is not really damaged."

"Maybe. But the main is ripped pretty badly, rudder is broken and I think the center board is probably floating off to Bermuda."

Sam stood.

"Well, let's see what we can do here. You rested enough?"

First, they disconnected the shrouds and stays from boat's deck and dragged the broken mast, boom and main sail up onto dry sand. Sam took the sail off the main and boom, laid it out on the beach and carefully folded it into a tight package.

"It might be worth stitching up," she said. They laid the mast and boom in parallel up against a dune, with Trav not much help with only one functional arm. They then returned to the boat, heaved it upside down to empty it of sea water, rolled it back and dragged it up high on the beach, pointing her bow northward. They both plopped down on the sand to catch their breath.

Trav picked up a broken shell and tossed it toward the water.

"I want to pay you for a new Flying Scot."

"Oh, don't be silly. It was an old boat."

"Well, I insist on paying you for the repairs, if that's what you decide to do."

"Let's not even think about that right now. You've got to get on the mend and then you need to head back home."

Trav didn't respond. Sam doodled in the sand between her outstretched legs. Still looking down she said, "Trav, I want to say something to you. And this might make you upset. We've gotten to know each other a bit, but basically we're just strangers passing in the night. If I make you mad, so be it."

Trav looked over at her, puzzled.

"I said I'm sorry about the boat."

"No, it's not that."

"What then?"

She turned and looked at him square on.

"You drink too much. I'm worried about you. You need to get that under control."

Trav looked out at the sea and said nothing for a long minute. He wasn't mad.

"Yeah, I know. I know," he said finally. He threw another shell, this time out as far as he could. "Actually," he said, "I think maybe I don't drink enough. I allow myself to sober up between drinks and then I see my sorry-ass life for what it is."

"Your sorry-ass life?" Sam challenged sharply.

"We talked about all my stuff the other night," Trav said. "I've lost people I love. I've got a dead twin. I've got a lost son. Now I've just been informed I'm an alcoholic."

Sam doodled again in the sand, then looked over at her boat and back at Trav.

"You don't believe in God, do you?"

"Of course I do!" Trav responded with vehemence. "How could I be so pissed at Someone I didn't believe existed?"

Sam looked out to sea, seemingly mesmerized. Finally she blinked and said, "Well, it's all a mystery, isn't it?"

"You got that right."

"Do you go to church?"

Trav waved out in front of him with his good arm. "That out there, the sea and the sand and the sky." He looked over at Sam. "That's my church."

Sam reached over to Trav and placed her hand on his good shoulder. "You know, I just think for a guy who is so mad at the Man Upstairs, seems odd that you've sure been saved a lot."

Trav looked at her, stunned.

"Excuse me?"

"You've been so locked in to your losses, but listening to your story the other night I heard..." She paused.

"You heard what?" Trav asked, an edge to his voice.

Sam began slowly.

"I heard that you, against all odds, were saved on the battlefield. Then I heard that, by a fluke or something, you were saved from dying in a helicopter crash."

"Well, that was..."

She went on.

"Then last month, you were maybe saved from a fatal car crash with your sister."

Trav broke in.

"No. No. If she had let me drive her..."

Sam wasn't finished.

"And there was your other little brush with death. When was that? Oh yes, yesterday afternoon, courtesy of Mother Nature. The crusty sorry-ass curmudgeon is saved again."

Trav was silent. *Saved? Saved?*

"And also," Sam said softly, not sure she should say the next thing. She looked up at the darkening evening sky. Then she did say it.

"And also, maybe you were saved the day you were born."

Trav slowly turned to face Sam, who continued her gaze straight ahead.

"The day I was born?" *How did she know?*

Sam shrugged nonchalantly. "I'm just saying."

Trav closed his eyes and contemplated what Sam had said.

*Saved? Saved a lot? Why?*

The predictable late afternoon breeze was gathering as the sun slowly sank toward the dunes behind them. A lone pelican, looking for one final morsel before the sun's rays blocked his view, spotted his prey just below the water's surface. It dove straight down in a dive-bombing plunge into the sea. Trav watched with amusement. Good luck, buddy, he thought.

He turned his attention back to the beach. Then he looked over at the stern of Sam's boat. B RACE ONE.

"I've been meaning to ask you," he said. "Why did you name the Scot B Race One?"

"I didn't. It was father's boat. He didn't name it that either."

"Huh?"

"Look. " Sam said, pointing to the stern of the boat. "Some of the letters are missing."

Trav saw the obvious odd space between the B and R and the second space between the E and the O. Missing letters.

"Do you do crossword puzzles?" Sam asked.

"Not much," Trav answered, still examining the stern. "I'm not getting it."

"I'll give you a hint. The name is three words and there are four letters missing."

Trav stared at B RACE ONE for a long time. He muttered, "Three words. Four letters missing. I still don't get it."

"I'll give you another hint. Last one. The name was most appropriate for your little venture yesterday afternoon."

Trav tried to run through letters and word combinations in his mind. He shook his head. "I give up."

"All his life, my father was religious. Even as a youth, his faith was rock solid. When he was given that old boat—brand-new then—he named her 'BY GRACE ALONE.' She pointed to the port side of the stern. The Y, the G, the A and the l are long gone. Floating to Europe maybe."

Trav pulled his legs up closed to his chest and rested his elbows on his knees. He took in a long deep breath and a longer slow exhale. Then he said, almost inaudibly, "By Grace Alone. I never would have gotten it."

"No, I don't suppose you would." She shifted over a bit closer to Trav, then added rather off-handedly, "It's mentioned one hundred and fifty-nine times in the Bible"

"What is?"

"The word grace."

They sat for a long time, both looking out to sea. Sam quietly broke the silence.

"I don't know much about you. But I know that you lived to grow up to be a man. You became the father your own father never was. You came back from war."

Trav's lower lip began to quiver. Sam reached over, careful not to touch his injured shoulder, and put her hand on his neck.

"And yesterday, somehow, Someone or Something allowed your foot to touch the bottom of the sea."

Trav's eyes filled with tears. His gaze over to B RACE ONE dissolved into a soft blur and he buried his head into his folded arms. Sam stroked the back of his neck.

"After my father died," she said, "I railed at God. I cried and I cursed Him and screamed at Him. For years, I did. The Bible says, 'The Lord giveth and Lord taketh Away.' And why? I think we're not supposed to know. I believe though that there is a higher power, a spirit, a Something there, call it what you will. He taketh away. But what he gives is, for me at least, by grace alone."

Trav slipped his good arm around Sam's waist and leaned his head on her shoulder and sobbed. In time, his crying subsided into to a soft silence and he whispered, "Thank you, my friend. I'm so tired of fighting with God. My anger has exhausted me."

Sam stroked his neck again.

"You're a good man, Traveler. A good man. Maybe you can surrender into this universe and end your own war and carry on."

# CHAPTER 28

## Leaving the Island

The car was all packed. Trav walked through the cottage one last time to make sure he had not left anything. He had decided to leave his booze in the kitchen as a welcome gift for the next renters. He stood in front of the sink and looked out the window to where Sam's Flying Scot once rested. A half empty bottle of vodka stood beside his two remaining bottles of wine. He stared at it. It stared back at him.

*Come on. One last farewell.*

He couldn't be expected to stop cold turkey. He would deal with all that when he got home.

So he sat one last time on the deck with a glass of vodka on the rocks. The morning was still young. Too early, maybe, for the sea gulls to food fight. Trav raised his glass to the glassy sea.

"So long, Mother Ocean. See you next time," he said out loud. He threw his head back and drained the last of the vodka.

He started to stand, but something prompted him to tarry for another minute. He rested his back against the rocking chair. Then something happened. Something odd. Maybe it was the effect of the vodka, but he didn't think so. Somehow, he felt—not thought—felt as though the ocean was god or at least part of god. More, he was a wave in that ocean. Not a discreet thing, not a separate person. Rather, like a wave, simply a pattern rolling inexorably through an inscrutable vastness. This feeling that had come upon him unbidden was deeply mysterious. But he liked it. He liked it very much. He stood now and looked one last time out at his precious friend, the deep blue sea, and smiled.

He passed back through the cottage and for the first and last time, locked the front door behind him and drove off. He stopped to say good bye to Homer and Gwen, dropped the key off at A Place at the Beach and headed for Sam's house.

He pulled to a stop just as Sam was heading out her front door, car keys in one hand and a satchel of books in the other. She looked up in surprise as Trav pressed the button that rolled down the passenger side window. Sam approached the car and leaned into the window, glancing at Trav's belongings piled in the back seat.

"Good morning."

"And top of the morning to you too."

"Where are you going?" she asked warily.

"I'm heading home. I came over to say goodbye."

Sam stepped back from the passenger side and marched around to the other side of the car, preparing her admonition as she did so.

"Traveler! What did the doctor tell you?"

"Umm. He said take care and take those pills if I needed to."

"Come on now, damn it!" she said, her brow furrowing. "He said specifically for you not to drive until he told you could take the sling off."

Trav rested his right hand on the steering wheel. "Well, that was kind of a..."

Sam interrupted him, "Did you call your wife?"

"Of course. We had a long talk last night. She's looking forward to having me home."

"Did you tell her you were driving from North Carolina to Pennsylvania with a dislocated shoulder in a sling?"

"Of course not."

"And you didn't tell her because?"

"Because there are times in a man's life, Samantha, when it is better to ask forgiveness after the fact rather than permission."

Sam stood upright, looking off in the distance, tapping her frustrated fingers on the roof of the car.

"I pity poor Martha. You really are untrainable. What would she do if she were here right now?"

Trav looked out through his front windshield and thought for a moment.

"She'd probably drive the car."

Sam drew in a deep, exasperated breath.

"Trav, I thought maybe you were going to stop doing dumb self-destructive things."

He looked up at her, trying to conceal his sense of mirth.

"I am, Sam. But I can't just stop cold turkey. You've got to get into it gradually."

Clearly, Sam was getting nowhere with her stubborn friend and she was not appreciating his humor. She surrendered and changed her tact. She hesitated, then leaned down again to the car window.

"Well," she said in a softer tone of voice, "do what you will. Please be safe. Let's stay in touch. Next time, bring Martha. That way, you might have a shot at an accident-free vacation."

"I will," Trav said, laughing and reaching over with his right hand and placing it on her forearm. "Sam," he said, changing his tone also, "I can't thank you enough for all you did. I mean it. You helped me more than you know." He moved his hand to the ignition, turned the key and looked back up to her.

"Bye, kiddo."

"Bye," she said softly.

As he pulled away, he saw her waving in the rearview mirror.

# CHAPTER 29

## The Surprise Party

Martha busied herself in the kitchen with the birthday cake while Spear and Eryn sat in the family room and chatted. She reflected on the last two weeks. Trav's escape to the island had done him some good, she thought. He seemed to be more on an even keel. His injuries were healing well. He was drinking much less. Mood seemed better and talking more positively about work and the firm. The sound of Trav's car pulling into the driveway caused her to scurry and call out in a stage whisper, "He's here. Go hide!"

Martha posted herself in front of the kitchen sink while Spear and Eryn hid against the wall in the family room. They heard the key slide into the front door lock and turn. The door opened.

"Hello."

"Hi," Martha called nonchalantly, "I'm in here."

As he stepped into the kitchen, Eryn, with Spear just behind her, sprung into view.

"Surprise! Happy birthday!"

The expression on Trav's face said it all. He clearly had no clue. Eryn moved forward with arms open to give her dad a big hug.

"Happy birthday, Pops."

"Wow! What a nice present to see you. When did you get here?"

"A couple of hours ago."

Trav moved to give Spear a man-to-man hug, then turned to Martha and hugged her.

"You stinker. You really got me."

Martha laughed.

"Well, it's not an extravagant celebration, but I wanted to do something."

"What could be better than a birthday with my three favorite people?" Trav caught himself, thinking of Daniel, then corrected his previous words, saying, "Three of my favorite people."

After a dinner of roast chicken, mashed potatoes and succotash, Trav's perennial favorite, Martha cleared the table and disappeared into the kitchen. A few minutes later she reappeared with the cake, on top of which were five full length candles and a stubby half-candle. They all sang the obligatory happy birthday song, after which Trav performed the obligatory extinguishing of the six flames. He watched the candles smoke.

"What's with the one little candle?

Martha laughed. "If I had put a candle on for each year, the fire department would show up. Each candle is a decade. Five and a half."

"Very clever, dear."

"Here are your birthday cards," Martha said, putting three envelopes on the table in front of Trav. "And," she added, "here is a letter from your island girlfriend."

Trav looked up at Martha.

"My girlfriend?"

Martha pointed down at the return name and address of the envelope. "Isn't that the gal on Okracoke Island you told me about?"

Trav looked at the envelope.

"Yep. That's her." He had to admit to himself that he had thought about Samantha more than once since returning home.

Eryn looked at her father.

"Your girlfriend?"

Trav simultaneously became a bit indignant and mirthful.

"Oh, for gosh sakes! She is *not* my girlfriend! She's a neighbor lady I met down at the beach. I wrecked and destroyed her sailboat and chose to ignore just about every piece of advice she offered. She did help a lot when I was injured and drove me to the hospital." Trav opted not to mention that she insisted he stay the night at her house. "She's a friend. Just a friend."

Trav opened the three birthday cards in front of him and laughed at all three. He then opened the letter from Sam and unfolded it. There was silence around the table which he knew Martha couldn't stand any longer.

"What does she say?"

Trav cleared his throat, then spoke out loud, pretending to read.

"My dearest Trav. I have been so miserable since you left. I long for your touch in the moonlight and our secret..."

Martha exploded. "What!" at which Trav tried to continue his pretend reading, but lost control with laughter. While Eryn looked on totally confused, Spear collapsed in laughter at the end of the table.

"...and our succulent kisses on the beach."

"Come on, Trav," Martha said, laughing herself now. "what does she say?"

Trav got control of himself, sort of, and started again.

"Her handwriting is hard to read. Okay, let's see. Okay.

> Dear Trav,
>
> I hope this finds you well and I hope your shoulder and legs and head are healing. Regarding the latter, it's that stubborn maverick element behind the cranium that I'm more worried about. Maybe your loving wife can find a remedy for you.

"Fat chance on that one," Martha muttered under her breath.

Trav looked up at Martha, then back down at Sam's lette,r searching for the place where he had stopped. He continued:

> Remember the word, my friend. The one that appears a hundred and fifty-nine times in the Bible.
> Hope you and Martha will come visit on Okracoke.
> Happy Birthday.
>
> All the best, Sam

"That's a sweet note," said Martha. "How did she know it was your birthday?"

"Oh, don't know," Trav deadpanned. "Maybe I mentioned it between kisses in the moonlight."

Spear and Eryn burst out laughing.

"Oh, stop!" said Martha, laughing at herself.

In fact, on his one-armed drive home, he had figured out that Sam must have surreptitiously read the letter from the hospital out on the porch when he was in the kitchen. But he wasn't sure he wanted to divulge that suspicion just then.

"I told her," he fibbed, "before I left the island that I wanted to get home in time for my birthday. She must have remembered because she said her brother's birthday was the same day."

Eryn then spoke up.

"What's with the word a hundred and fifty-nine times in the Bible?"

Trav looked over at her, then at Martha, then Spear. When he arrived home, he and Martha had had a long, wonderful visit together in the family room, and he had told her all about his time on the island. The fishing, the walks, the loneliness, Homer and Gwen and the dinner party, and meeting Sam. He told her about Sam's boat and the storm and his brush with death. But he had not shared with her the complicated tale of the boat's name, his talk with Sam on the beach that evening, his tears and his epiphany. Trav had changed, but he was still a guy and still a stubborn maverick kind of guy, and there was a part of his soul he continued to guard closely.

Trav looked back at his daughter.

"The word, sweetheart, is grace." He paused then decided he wanted to tell the whole story.

He took a small sip of his wine, then moved into the story of B RACE ONE and the actual name, what Sam had said that day and how he came to see, really for the first time in his life, that his story was not only about loss but about salvation. Being saved. Being saved over and over. There was a lingering silence in the room.

Finally, Martha, in a soft voice asked, "Why didn't you tell me about this when you first came home?"

Trav shrugged.

"I don't know, honestly. I just..." He searched inside for the answer to Martha's question. "I just...It was just too close to the bone somehow. It was so powerful, but I was still trying to think about it and figure things out then."

Spear, who had been uncharacteristically quiet through the evening, spoke.

"Trav, you have been trying—trying too hard—to figure everything out. Sometimes, I think it's better just to let things flow and see them and enjoy them."

Martha turned her head toward the front hall, asking of no one in particular,

"Did you hear something?"

"What?" said Trav. "Hear what?"

"Sounded like someone was at the front door."

The four were quiet for a moment. Then they heard the knock. Trav pushed his chair back, put his napkin on the table and headed for the front hall. As he reached for the brass knob, there was another knock. Trav opened the door. Seeing the person before him, he stood frozen in stunned silence.

"Daniel!" he whispered.

Martha called from the dining room.

"Who is it, honey?"

Daniel was dressed in dirty blue jeans with a ripped hole at the knee and an oversized, faded Army surplus jacket. Above his scraggly beard were two tired, expressionless blue eyes. He looked up at his father.

"Hey, Pops."

Martha called again to Trav, who was oblivious to her. He stepped forward, wanting to hold his son and hug him. But he resisted the impulse. Instead he swung the big wooden door open wider and said simply, "Come on in."

Martha entered the hall behind Trav. Her eyes widened and her jaw dropped. "Oh, my...!" Unlike her husband, she had no reluctance to follow her impulse and threw her arms around Daniel who, fighting to breathe against his mother's tight embrace, managed to say, "Hey, Mom," as he put his hands on her back.

Eryn came up behind them.

"Hey, bro. We've all been worried about you."

"Hey, Sis," Daniel answered, breaking the embrace.

Martha reached for Daniel's hand and pulled him into the living room toward the dining room.

"Come on. You're just in time for some of Dad's birthday cake."

Trav slid a fifth chair up to the table as Martha discreetly grabbed the wine bottle and headed for the kitchen. Daniel sat and proceeded to devour the slice of cake and tall glass of milk in front of him.

"How did you get here?" Trav asked.

"Hitchhiked," Daniel answered through a mouthful of cake. He was not talkative, except to provide clipped, often vague, answers to direct questions.

"Hung out different places."

"Worked some at a mall."

It had been almost three months since their last communication with Daniel. Days and weeks of worrying and anger and resignation. What to say? What to ask? What to require of him now? After virtually inhaling a plate of chicken and mashed potatoes and a second piece of cake, Daniel said, "I'm really tired. Can I go upstairs and sleep?"

Martha and Trav looked at each other.

"Sure," they said simultaneously.

Trav, watching his son stand and walk out of the room, felt a rush of relief and at the same time a sense of emptiness. The boy was home and he was safe, but this was not the reunion he had envisioned. He reached for the birthday cake and looked around the table.

"Anyone?"

# CHAPTER 30

## *Trav's Letter*

Ann Sample walked past the small *A Place at the Beach* sign hanging on a curbside post and fished for her keys to unlock the door of the office. She stepped over the mail that had cascaded through the slot onto the floor inside. She took off her coat, made a pot of coffee and gathered the mail, which she would go through and sort at her desk. Near the bottom of the pile was a letter addressed by hand to Ms. Samantha Brewer c/o A Place at the Beach.

She finished sorting the mail, went to the little back room to pour herself a mug of coffee, returned to her desk and made a phone call that went to voice mail.

> *Hey Sam, it's Ann on the island. Wanted to let you know that a letter for you came here to the office. I can forward it to you, but I'm guessing you're coming out here next week for Thanksgiving. If I don't hear from you, I'll assume that's the case and just hold the letter for you. All the best. Bye.*

Trav had wanted Sam's address and had searched Martha's desk and the kitchen area for her birthday letter to him and had not found it. Reluctant to ask Martha where the letter was, he finally decided to just send his letter to the real estate office on the island.

❦❦

It was the Tuesday before Thanksgiving. The car ferry from Swanquarter on the mainland eased into the old brown piling slip on the island. The ferry's two-man crew made secure with the large cable-laced hemp lines, lowered the steel ramp and signaled to the small cluster of cars and pick-ups that they were free to drive off. The third vehicle off the ferry was a Jeep Wrangler with no side doors. Sam had intended to drive straight to her cottage but remembered Ann's phone message as she neared the real estate office.

Ann and Sam chatted and caught up for a few minutes, after which Sam departed, letter in hand. She also had intended once again to go directly to her cottage until she noticed the sender's name and address in the upper left-hand corner of the envelope. She pulled out of the small parking lot and headed for the coast road, stopping at a gas station on the way for a soft drink.

She was fairly certain the Padgette cottage would be closed up for the season and, pulling into the sandy drive by the front door, saw that her guess was correct. On Veteran's Day, a vicious nor'easter had slammed into the island, altering the shape of dunes, blowing shutters off houses and flooding portions of the island. The locals had already named it the Eleven –Eleven Storm.

Sam walked around to the ocean side of the cottage, climbed the few steps, the bottom one of which was now buried in sand, and onto to the deck. She brushed storm-deposited sand off the side table and off one of the rocking chairs. She sat and rocked gently, twisting the cap off her Dr. Pepper, surveying the scene before her. No boats at sea. No birds in the air. No beachcombers in sight. Solitude. Sam liked this kind of solitude. She looked down at the letter in her lap and opened it.

> *Dear Sam,*
>
> *I lost your home address and had to resort to the real estate office delivery services. Hope this gets to you.*
>
> *I am sorry it has taken me so long to get this letter off to you. It's taken a while to readjust. (I keep waking up, looking out the window expecting to see the beach!)*

*Thank you for your birthday note. It was a real surprise and within minutes of reading, we all got another surprise. There was a knock on the front door. It was Daniel. He's been home almost three weeks now and we've had some rough patches with him.*

*On Veterans Day, he and I drove down to Washington, D.C. and went to the Wall. I introduced him to Vince and for the first time in my life, I talked with my son about Vietnam and about my dreams and about my sadness. It was a good talk. Probably more meaningful for me than him. But it was good.*

*Who knows where he is going to head with his own life, but it seems, at least for now, that he is intent on changing directions, as am I. You will be interested to know we have found a father-son activity to do together: attend AA meetings. Yes, really! One day at a time!*

*I have thought a lot about our talk together on the beach after the storm. As you said, I was so locked in on what had been lost, not what had been saved. "Was blind, but now I see..." I can't thank you enough.*

*Martha and I have talked about coming down to the island next summer. I know I can't be trusted to skipper By Grace Alone; but if you'll take us out for a sail, we'll take you out for dinner.*

*Speaking of sailing, I hope the enclosed will cover your boat repair expenses.*

*Happy Thanksgiving.*

*Trav*

Sam slowly reread the letter then stepped down off the deck and walked to the water's edge. For a long moment, she studied the check made out to her for one thousand dollars. Then she tore it into small pieces and threw them into the surf. Sam put the letter in her pocket, turned her face to the sun and smiled.

# CHAPTER 31

## The Long Way Home

The sharp brilliance of October's foliage had faded into the muted collage of the remaining leaves of November. Eryn was back on campus and plowing happily through her fall semester. Trav, Martha and Daniel were settling into an edgy, not altogether comfortable routine. Through some back-channel prodding by Trav, the principal at the local high school had allowed Daniel to take two senior level classes in the morning, after which he walked to Petermann's Hardware for his part time job that his father had also quietly secured for him.

Martha had reluctantly agreed to allow their son to live at home.

"Okay," she had said to both Daniel and Trav, "I'll go along with this for the time being on one condition." Daniel looked warily over at his mother. She continued, "That you go to AA meetings at least three times a week and that you get a sponsor and that you demonstrate to us that you are serious about this."

Daniel looked down at his black sneakers, then out at the garden scene through the family room bay window. Trav watched Martha watching him, then asked Daniel, "Do you agree?"

Daniel, still looking out at the garden, answered in a quiet, clear voice, "I agree."

The last Saturday in November was unseasonably warm. Martha regarded Trav across from her at their small kitchen table.

"More coffee?"

Trav looked up from the sports section of the newspaper and handed his mug across to her.

"Sure."

Martha stood and turned to the kitchen counter, reaching for the coffee pot.

"So you and Daniel are having lunch with Spear today?"

"Uh huh," Trav mumbled, still reading.

"What's that all about?" Martha handed Trav his refill and sat back down.

"Thanks," Trav said, folding his newspaper and placing it on the kitchen window sill. Trav wanted to know his son, to know what he was thinking, what he was planning, and he thought a discussion with a third party, especially a kindly gentle soul like Spear, might produce more information from Daniel than his father could extract on his own. But he didn't share this strategy with Martha. Instead, he said, "Well, Spear's just been asking about Daniel. He hasn't seen him except the day he came home. We, Spear and I, just thought it might be fun, kind of a father-son-guys outing."

Since he had been back home, Daniel had been relatively good about getting up and starting his day and generally being cooperative. Martha and Trav had decided that on weekends he could sleep in and that morning, sleep in he did. It was almost noon when he appeared in the kitchen.

"Morning, young man," Martha said cheerily.

"Morning," Daniel replied, not quite so cheery. "What's for breakfast?"

"It's almost noon," I thought you and Dad were going to Mr. Robespiere's for lunch."

"Oh, yeah," Daniel said, opening the refrigerator door. "What's that all about?"

"I don't know, really. I think Spear just invited the two of you. You'll have fun."

Trav and Daniel walked the loop path together. As they stepped through Spear's back gate, their host opened his door and walked toward them.

"Hi," Spear said, smiling broadly. "It's the McGale men."

Trav reached for Spear's outstretched hand.

"Hello, my friend."

Daniel dutifully stepped forward. "Hi, Mr. Robespiere. Thanks for inviting me."

"You are most welcome. Come in."

They dined at a small table Spear had moved just for the occasion into his den. The serving was grilled cheese sandwiches, Spear's homemade potato salad and Cokes. The two men bantered back and forth as Daniel concentrated on his first meal of the day, which he acknowledged was "mighty good." Spear cleared the empty plates and disappeared into his kitchen. He reappeared proudly with a plate piled high with his home-made chocolate chip cookies.

"Oooooh," purred Trav, reaching for one.

Spear sat. As he placed his napkin in his lap, he turned to Daniel.

"So, Daniel, you're getting along alright these days? School? Your job at the hardware store?"

"Yep," Daniel said. "It's going along pretty good."

Pretty well, not pretty good, Trav thought, but restrained himself from saying it out loud.

"And what are you focusing on now?" Spear asked.

Daniel finished chewing his mouthful of cookie.

"First priority right now is to stay clean. I'm going to meetings."

Trav watched his son closely. *Was this just a line he knew his father wanted to hear? Was he serious?*

"Can't disagree with that," Spear said. "And school?"

"Yeah, school," Daniel said with little enthusiasm. "I definitely want to finish high school. I'm taking classes now."

"Yes," said Spear, "your dad told me." He took a sip of his Coke, then continued. "You know, Daniel, you are a lot like your old man here, a real curmudgeon."

Daniel was puzzled.

"What's a curmudgeon?"

"A curmudgeon?" Spear said, " Well, it's like a rascal, only not as high class."

Trav could see that Daniel didn't quite catch the humor. Spear pushed on. "So, young man, let me pose to you a hypothetical question." Daniel looked expressionless at his father's old friend. "Let's say, Daniel, we are sitting here a year from now, maybe a year and a half, and you have straightened yourself out with the drugs and the booze and you've finished high school. By then you're what, nineteen, maybe twenty. What will you be thinking of doing?"

Trav was enjoying himself, listening to someone else try to probe Daniel's thoughts and plans. But he was not prepared for what was to come next. Daniel slowly chewed his cookie, then swallowed. He glanced at his father and turned back to Spear.

"Not sure really, but I've been thinking." Daniel paused and took some more Coke. "I've been thinking I might join the Marines."

Trav's eyes opened wide. His jaw dropped. He started to say something to his son, but Spear held his hand, palm out, toward Trav, signaling 'Let me handle this.'

"Marines, huh?" Spear asked nonchalantly.

"Maybe," said Daniel, "I'm not too sure really. Just thinking about it."

Trav was aching to ask more about this new revelation, but forced himself to wait until he was alone with Daniel.

&#x2767;

Lunch was over. Father and son said their thank yous and goodbyes to Spear. As Trav pulled the back gate behind him, he suggested to Daniel, "Let's take the long way around."

"Why?"

"Just because. It's a beautiful afternoon."

Daniel was learning to pick his battles and recognized that this little one was not worth the fight. The day had warmed. High cirrus clouds drifted slowly overhead. They walked side by side in silence. Ahead, a black wrought iron bench came into view.

"Let's sit for a minute," Trav suggested.

Another small battle not worth the fight. Daniel bowed his head in mild frustration and took a seat. Trav picked up a small branch that was on the bench and sat down. He slowly, pensively snapped the branch, tossing small pieces out onto the path. Daniel looked straight ahead. Another piece of branch arced out onto the path.

"That was a good lunch," Trav said finally.

"Yeah, delicious."

"Spear's a nice friend. One of my closest."

"Yeah, I like him. He's a good cook. I'll give him that."

"Good cook, indeed."

The last piece of branch hit the path, bounced once and stopped. Trav looked down at his feet for something else to toss.

"We haven't really talked, you and I, since you came home."

Daniel recrossed his legs, laying an ankle on a knee.

"Well," he said, not meanly, "what's to talk about?"

Trav looked up and out across the path.

"For starters, I'd like to hear about why you ran away...twice...from Burson-Mann."

Daniel was quiet. Then he said, "I know they're trying to help the students up there, but they treated us like children. Do this. Do that. What are you thinking? Why are you thinking that? I just couldn't take it after a while." He looked over at his father. "I'm young, but I'm not stupid. I know I've got a problem and I appreciate your help, you and Mom, but I've got to do it myself."

Daniel turned and again looked straight ahead, squinting into the November sun. Trav regarded his son for a long time. He saw his two-day-old scruff of a beard on his chin and cheeks. He studied Daniel's solid shoulders and the muscles in his neck. He is no longer a boy, he thought. As much as his heart resisted, Trav knew he had to let go.

"You're right. You've got to do it."

"Yep."

Trav wanted to ask the other question. He flashed on that night and the hill and Lanzi. He heard the unmistakable thrumping of the helicopter blades. He saw Vince's blood on his hands. He wanted to ask Daniel about his plans. Trav thought better of it. He hesitated and then changed his mind again.

"What's this about the Marines?"

Daniel looked down at his hands.

"I'm just thinking about it."

"I would have thought you might have discussed it with me."

Daniel looked over at his father.

"You mean the way you discussed joining the Marines with your father?"

That stung. Stung hard. Daniel knew, because Trav had told him once that he didn't say a word to his parents about the Marines until after he had signed up.

"At least I'm talking to you about it before the fact,."

Trav looked over at Daniel.

"You are. You are indeed."

Daniel pulled his cell phone out of his pocket to check the time.

"Geez, I gotta get to my afternoon shift. I'm gonna head back the short way."

As Daniel started to stand, Trav impulsively reached for him, putting his arm around Daniel's shoulder, pulling him close.

"I love you, buddy."

Daniel did not resist the embrace.

"I love you too. I gotta go."

Trav stood and watched his son walking, then jogging down the path. The Fall leaves, those still clinging to their branches and those already on the ground, were all a soft golden yellow. He watched Daniel until he disappeared around the bend. *Let go*, Trav whispered to himself. *Let go. Let go. Let go.* He continued to stare at the now empty path.

*Maybe he'll be as lucky in life as I have been. Maybe someone, someday, when the time is right, will tell him about grace.*

Trav kicked at the golden leaves and the pieces of branch on the path, turned and began to walk in the opposite direction. He would take the long way home.

CPSIA information can be obtained
at www.ICGtesting.com
Printed in the USA
FFOW01n1855150715
15178FF